ANGEL FALLS
ANGEL FALLS SERIES BOOK ONE

CHARLENE TESS
JUDI THOMPSON

Copyright © 2019
by Charlene Tess and Judi Thompson
All rights reserved.

No part of this publication may be reproduced, distributed, or transmitted in any form or by any means, including photocopying, recording, or other electronic or mechanical methods, without the prior written permission of the publisher, except as permitted by U.S. copyright law. For permission requests, contact novelsbyTessThompson@gmail.com.

The story, all names, characters, and incidents portrayed in this production are fictitious. No identification with actual persons (living or deceased), places, buildings, and products is intended or should be inferred.

*To our father, whose unconditional love and gentle guidance,
gave us our wings.*
Kenneth Richard Bourland (1916-2008)

ACKNOWLEDGMENTS

We appreciate our talented cousin who suggested the title of the book. You're the best, Chaz.

Thanks to our brother, Casey Bourland, who answered our questions about guns. All mistakes are ours.

Our heartfelt thanks go out to our first readers including Jerry Tess, Roger Thompson, Nancy Johnson, Chaz Bourland, Carolyn Wilhelm, and Shar Faison. We really appreciate the comments and the suggestions.

PART I

CHAPTER 1

The low growl followed by deep, rapid barks startled Maggie, and her head shot up from the pile of bills she had been shuffling through for most of the afternoon. Pushing back her chair, she watched as the dog clawed at the door.

A sting of alarm prickled Maggie's skin. This dog did not bark or growl without a reason. Even when she'd found him struggling to walk across the campground to search for food near the empty garbage can, he'd stood his ground, trembled, and wagged his tail. At that moment, she had fallen in love with the skinny, malnourished animal whose backbone protruded through the long, dirty layers of matted black and white hair. The name Boney seemed to fit.

"What is it, boy?" she said as she opened the desk drawer and pulled out her loaded revolver. She shoved it into her waistband and pulled a shotgun down from the rack on the wall. She heard the shuffle of her great-grandmother's feet in the hall and turned to see the older woman reaching for the remaining shotgun.

"Bella, you stay here. It's probably nothing."

"No, Chica. Something is out there. Boney's no fool dog."

"Please wait and let me look."

The old woman nodded and shrugged her shoulders. "*Muchaca terca*. Hardheaded girl. Exactly like your mama."

Maggie smiled, grabbed her jacket off the peg and opened the door. Boney ran out into a cloud of dust while dodging a dozen frightened horses. "Ah, hell," she spat. "It's the horses, Bella. They're out of the pen. I'm going to close the main gate so they can't get to the road." She looked up and spotted a rusty pickup truck trailing dust as it raced away. This was no accident, she thought. Someone had let them out.

The early October weather was turning colder, and long afternoon shadows spread across the thirsty soil. She glanced up toward the mountains where she usually saw snow-covered peaks, but today bare rocks shone in the fading light.

A small figure bobbed up and down as it made its way down the deer trail. Maggie squinted and lifted her palm to shield her eyes. It wasn't the right shape for a deer and was more likely a bear looking for water or food. She took a couple of steps back, focused her eyes on the descending figure, and clutched her long gun tightly. Then, she caught a glint of red between the trees. It wasn't an animal. It was a man.

Maggie wasn't a large woman, and she knew she would be no match physically for a man intent on harm. The incident with the horses was only a fraction of the mischief she believed her ex-husband had caused. She didn't think he would send someone to harm her, but she wasn't taking any chances. Her marksmanship more than compensated for her small stature. She was an excellent shot and didn't believe she would lose any sleep over putting a bullet through someone if it meant protecting her great-grandmother and their property.

The horses had settled down after their initial scare and were milling around by the barn. She needed to get them back into the pen before nightfall but didn't dare take her eyes off the figure of a person rapidly making his way down the mountain. She was sure now that it was a man. A large man with long, shaggy hair and a full beard.

She glanced back at her great-grandmother and saw the heavy shotgun resting in Bella's arms. "Someone is coming. Go back inside until I find out what he wants."

Maggie watched the determined scowl spread across her face and knew the words were wasted. "All right then, but at least stay up there on the porch. You'll know if I need help."

The scowl remained firmly plastered on Bella's face, but at least she wasn't moving toward the steps, Maggie thought. Her Bella had a spine of steel and the courage of ten men, but unfortunately, age and crippling arthritis greatly limited her physically.

Boney darted up to the porch and then back to Maggie with his tongue lolling from side to side. His eyes were fixed on the approaching figure.

The man was now about a hundred yards away. He wore a red plaid shirt, denim pants, a baseball cap, and a backpack. He didn't appear to have a weapon and put both of his hands up as he approached her.

"Sorry, ma'am, didn't mean to frighten you."

Maggie lowered the gun and studied the stranger standing in front of her. He was tall. Well over six feet, with a lean, raw-boned face and striking blue eyes. She licked her lips and pulled her long dark hair behind her ears. "Where did you come from?"

He pointed back toward the mountain and said, "Up there."

"That's obvious. But that's national forest land on the other side. We don't get many strangers walking down from the wilderness. As a matter of fact, you're the only one."

"What is this place?" He looked around at the rows of compact cabins, the barn and horse pens, and at the older woman standing on the porch of a large log home.

"Cielo Verde. That's Green Heaven in Spanish."

She was surprised when he said, "I know what it means. This a ranch or something?"

"No, it's a lodge and campground, and it's my turn to ask questions."

He shrugged, and she noticed the shadows under his eyes. It was impossible to tell his age because of the scruffy beard and mustache. He could be anywhere from his middle twenties to late forties. She stepped back a couple of feet and looked him up and down. "You look like something that walked off an eighties Grisly Adams movie set, and you stink like it too." If what she said offended him, he didn't show it.

"Now, let's try again. I know you came from up there." She pointed and sighed. "I've been watching for the last few minutes. I want to know what are you doing here on my property?"

"This is where the trail led me."

Maggie wanted to stomp her feet and scream. Instead, she calmly said, "Are you lost? People don't usually come here unless the lodge is their destination. We're tucked in here backed up to the mountain with the lake on the other side. Only one way in and one way out."

"Obviously not," he said and smiled.

He had a nice smile, and Maggie thought he probably didn't show it often. She waited for him to speak again and when he did it was to say, "No, I'm not lost."

Once more she waited, and when it was apparent he wasn't going to elaborate she asked the only logical question. "Then you're here for a visit? To stay at the lodge? This is the off-season, and we rarely get any guests this time of year. We're down to a skeleton staff now and have none of the amenities."

"No, I'm only passing through. But I'd appreciate it if I could fill my canteen." He reached down and patted Boney's head and scratched under his chin. "Nice dog."

Maggie watched the man's large hand stroke her dog and suddenly realized that Boney had not barked. This man was a stranger, a large, scary-looking stranger, and the dog was acting like his best friend.

They walked toward the house where a green hose lay coiled around a faucet already covered for the first freeze. Maggie turned it on and watched as the stranger filled the dark, olive-green bottle that looked like it was a reject from an army surplus store. He capped it and swung the strap over his shoulder.

Maggie held out her hand and said, "I'm Magdalena Morales, and this is my great-grandmother Bella Morales."

"Ma'am," he said looking at Bella.

When he didn't offer his name, the exasperation must have shown on her face because he quickly cleared his throat as if it hurt to talk and said, "I'm Russell Murphy. Thank you for the water."

He turned toward the dirt road and stopped when Bella said, "You know horses, Mr. Murphy?"

"Can't say as I do."

"Are you afraid of them?"

"I don't think so. I've never thought about it."

"My great-granddaughter could use some help."

His grin flashed briefly. "I was wondering if you always kept your horses on the front lawn?"

Maggie's mouth dropped open, and she snapped it shut before she could comment. That string of words was more than the man had said since he arrived, and if she was not mistaken, he had made a joke.

"No, we usually keep them in that pen, but lately we've had a string of vandalism and just plain meanness. Right before I saw you, someone opened the gate and let them out," Maggie said.

"Can you help Maggie get them back where they belong? It would be a favor to me, and we can offer you a free meal for your trouble," Bella said.

Russell nodded. "Show me what you need me to do, Magdalena."

～

GETTING the horses back into the pen wasn't as hard as Russell thought it would be. For the most part, they were eager to get to the piles of hay that Magdalena threw into the feed bins. The light was fading quickly, but he could still see her dark curly hair bouncing on her shoulders, and he admired the way her trim figure fit nicely into her jeans.

Her great-grandmother had called her Maggie, but she looked more like her given name Magdalena. With her olive skin and her flashing brown eyes, she was the image of a Spanish dancer. He took his eyes off her, but not quick enough to see the excited horse's leg kick backward and strike a painful blow to his knee.

He cringed and sucked in his breath. *Damn*, he thought, *that hurt*. The first time he'd looked at a woman in months, and he'd been punished for it. Served him right. He stood up straight and hoped he could push through the pain. He'd had his share of bruises and breaks growing up and had become adept at fooling teachers and coaches.

Maggie shut the gate and put a padlock she'd taken out of the barn through the chain. "That should take care of that," she said wiping the rust from the chain on her pants.

It was full-on dark now as stars began to spread across the sky. He loved the outdoors here in the Sangre de Cristo Mountains of New Mexico. They were his solace and his refuge. When he looked at the sky, he could almost forget.

He took a step toward Maggie and said, "I was wondering if I could stay in your barn tonight? It's too dark to set up camp down the road anywhere."

"You're welcome to use one of the cabins. They're quite comfortable and have hot, running water. We even have soap and shampoo," she laughed. "Let me go get the keys to the ATV, and I'll run you over there. You can get cleaned up, and I'll drop by in an hour and take you back to the house for supper."

"What about your great-grandmother? Will she mind if I stay?"

"Oh, I don't think so. I believe for some reason you made a good impression on our dog. He didn't bark or growl at you, even though he doesn't like men as a whole. I'm pretty sure one must have abused him." She smiled and said, "So you are definitely an enigma. And as for Bella, she'd have run you off instead of asking for your help. I guess you could say she's an enigma too. You'll see. She's a little different."

~

RUSSELL DIDN'T RECOGNIZE the face he saw in the mirror. He'd lost some weight, and his cheeks looked hollow. He didn't have a razor or scissors, but he did have a relatively clean change of clothes he'd washed in one of the small towns he'd passed through.

He moaned aloud as the nearly scalding water fell on his head and across his shoulders. He soaped his hair and body three times before he felt clean. Somehow, what Magdalena thought was important to him. He knew it shouldn't be since he would be leaving early in the morning, and he would never see her again.

He wondered what the story was. Why were two women running this lodge all alone? Where were all of the workers? Even in the off-season, there should have been people to do repairs and upkeep. He wasn't going to ask. He had no intention of getting involved or learning more about vandals and meanness.

He looked down at his knee and the dark red mark and knew that by morning it would be stiff and swollen. After he left, he'd have to find a good valley to settle in for the next few days until it got better. Thank the Lord he didn't have to walk up to the house, and the sooner he got away from those haunting Spanish eyes, the better off he would be.

∾

MAGGIE SAW a different man standing in the cabin doorway. This Russell Murphy was clean and smelled like fresh mint. He had changed clothes, and she could see that without the coat and backpack, even though he was thin, he was a large man. She unconsciously took a step closer. "Wow, you clean up pretty good."

"You do too."

Maggie had changed into a clean pair of denim jeans and a black and white checked flannel shirt and black winter vest. She'd looked at everything in her closet and then finally pulled out the closest blouse. She didn't care what he thought. Why should she? He was a stranger, and for all she knew he could be a serial killer or worse. But all those thoughts were lost when she looked up into his blue eyes. Bella would say they were old eyes. That he was an old soul.

Maggie saw him wince when he stepped down from the four-wheeler and walked toward the steps of the main house. "You okay?"

"What?"

"You're limping?"

"I'm fine. I twisted my leg a little, that's all. No problem."

"Okay, if you say so." She opened the door to the smell of roasted chiles and garlic. "I hope you like green chile stew. Bella is a master in the kitchen. Me, not so much."

"Mija, that's not true. I taught you well. Please sit down, Mr. Murphy, here across from me."

"You have a beautiful log home, Mrs. Morales."

Maggie looked at the home she had lived in most of her life. It had tall ceilings that gave it an impressive feeling and huge logs that drew attention to the stone fireplace and large windows along one side of the room. But the great room still had a homey feel, and the antler chandelier over the oak table gave off a warm glow. She looked at Russell while she ladled the stew into large soup bowls. He seemed impressed as his eyes roamed the room.

"My husband's family has been in this valley for generations. Sadly, Maggie is the last of the Morales line. My son Miguel passed in Vietnam. His brother Ernesto's heart gave out, and we lost him earlier this year, and Maggie's mother is gone now too. I came here as a young bride, but of course, the house was smaller then and has since been renovated. Where do you come from, Mr. Murphy?"

"Please call me Russell, and this stew is delicious."

"The chile's not too hot for you?"

"No, it's fine. I like it when it makes me sweat. I noticed the red ones hanging outside. Do you use them for cooking or for decoration?"

Maggie couldn't help but notice how he had skillfully

not answered Bella's question and steered the conversation in another direction.

"We let them dry and then grind them up into chile powder. Which is your favorite?"

"Oh, I'm easy to please. I'll eat most anything that's put in front of me. That was really good, ladies. I thank you for your hospitality and for trusting a stranger." He put his napkin on the table and stood. "I've got to get an early start in the morning. I'd better get some sleep."

Bella reached across the table and took his hand. "Do you mind?" she said pulling his arm forward forcing him to sit back down.

"Mind?"

"Your hand. May I see it?"

"Sure, I guess."

"Fine strong hands and a good lifeline," Bella said. "Stubborn, like my girl. You have secrets, Mr. Murphy, and ghosts in your past and guilt. You have so much guilt."

Russell jerked his hand back from Bella and stood almost toppling the chair over. "What are you, a witch?"

Bella did not reply. Her eyes were dark and unfathomable.

"Something like that," Maggie said, smiling.

CHAPTER 2

Maggie shivered and closed the door on the crisp, frosty morning and rubbed her hands together. Hooking her jacket on a peg, she made her way to the kitchen. The horses seemed calm enough this morning, and everything outside looked relatively normal. "Good morning, Bella," she said spotting her great-grandmother sitting at the kitchen table.

"You look tired, mija. What's the matter?"

Maggie sat down and closed her eyes while warming her hands on a steaming cup of coffee. Her mind flashed back to the dream. The same dream she'd had for months. A young girl with brown curls ran toward her while flashing deep dimples and perfect little teeth as a smile spread across her beautiful face. She couldn't have been more than three or four years old as she ran giggling through the pines. Maggie picked her up and said, "I love you, Emma."

"I love you, Mama. When can I see you? Can you hurry please?"

The dream never changed. Maggie always woke up smiling and then felt empty when she realized it wasn't real.

"Yesterday was long and stressful what with Murphy showing up and the horses getting loose. And the bills, Bella. I don't know how we're going to make it. These last two seasons have really hurt."

"And what else? You have your dream again?"

"Yes, I did. It's nice until I wake up. I don't understand why I keep dreaming about that child. It's as if she's real."

"If you let me read the cards, perhaps I can help."

"No. I don't want to know my future, at least not right now. I'd rather stumble around in ignorance. I might not like what you tell me." Maggie got up from the table and warmed a tortilla over the gas flame on the stove and added egg and sausage.

"Go take a couple of those to our guest. He doesn't look as if he eats often enough."

"He's probably already gone. He said …" Maggie stopped and turned to look at Bella. "He's still here, isn't he?"

"How would I know?"

"Right," Maggie said and slapped two burritos onto aluminum foil and wrapped them tightly. "You like him, don't you?"

"I can see that he needs help. You're good at helping people, mija."

"I called the sheriff last night."

"You think he's a criminal?"

"No, not about Murphy. About the horses and the other damage."

"Bah, that big-bellied fool of a sheriff won't do anything about what's going on around here."

"I know it won't do any good, but I needed to have a record of my call on file in case we need to make an insurance claim in the future."

Bella grunted and tapped the tarot cards on the table. "You go see to our guest. Maybe you'll change your mind later about a reading."

Russell Murphy was outside wearing only a short sleeve t-shirt as he placed a large aspen log on the chopping block. He looked good, Maggie thought. Real good.

"By the way you talked, I thought you would have already headed out this morning," Maggie said as she stepped down from the ATV.

"I thought I'd chop some wood for that big, inviting fireplace you've got up at the house. Nights are cold now, so I imagine a fire would be nice for you and Bella."

"I'm sorry about last night. My great-grandmother tends to get into people's business. She didn't mean any harm and had only good intentions."

"That's okay. What she said was quite a shock, even if it was crazy talk."

Maggie knew Bella's track record was mostly accurate, but she wisely kept that comment to herself. "Here, I brought you some breakfast."

Russell pushed the log off and sat on the tree stump. "What's the story around here? Why are you and Bella here alone?"

Before she could answer, Maggie heard a car approaching. She looked back toward the road and cursed when she realized it was her ex-husband, Lyman O'Dell, in his shiny, black Land Rover.

"I'll be right back," she said. "I've got to take care of a pesky piece of trash."

"Morning, sweetheart," Lyman said. "I hear you had a little problem with the horses last night."

"And how would you know that?"

"The sheriff told me. Since I'm the mayor, anything that happens to my constituents is my concern, so he brought it to my attention."

"I'm sure you didn't tell him that you were the cause of that little problem, and I'm not your constituent. The lodge isn't within city limits."

"Sweetheart, I don't know why you've come up with this silly notion that I have anything to do with your troubles. Why would I want to cause you problems?"

"So I will admit defeat and let you buy our property."

"I confess. I do want this fine prime land. It's too much for you and Bella to handle anymore with your grandpa gone and all."

"Yeah," Maggie spat out the words, "especially since you've hired all the able-bodied men in the county. How am I supposed to get anyone to work for me when you're offering ridiculously high hourly wages?"

"That's capitalism for you, sweetheart. Supply and demand."

"If you call me *sweetheart* one more time, I'm going to let Boney loose on you. For the last time, I am not going to sell you my land. Not while I am still breathing."

Lyman reached down and grabbed Maggie's arm causing Boney to emit a low-pitched growl followed by a series of loud, vicious barks as he lunged toward the man. Lyman let go of her arm and hurried toward his vehicle.

"You better watch that dog, Maggie," he yelled. "He bites me, and I'll sue you."

Maggie saw Russell limping toward her and heard him ask, "Is there a problem?"

"No, no problem. Mr. O'Dell was leaving, weren't you, Lyman?"

Lyman jumped in the car and rolled down the window. "I mean it, Maggie. You're not going to be able to hold out much longer. I'll add another ten thousand to my offer, but after this week that's off the table. I'd hate to see anything happen to you or this property."

"Is that a threat, Mister?" Russell said.

"Who the hell is this, Maggie? Some derelict looking for a handout?"

"I'm Russell Murphy, and I'm here to tell you if you speak to Ms. Morales like that again I'm going to punch your pearly, white teeth down your throat. We derelicts are used to fighting dirty."

∼

RUSSELL WATCHED the fancy SUV drive off the property with Boney following close behind until the car reached the main road. Russell turned around to face a frowning Maggie.

"I could have handled him myself. I didn't need you to come riding up on your white horse to rescue me."

"Who is that jerk?"

"He is the illustrious mayor of our nearest town, Angel Falls, and he's my ex-husband. His name is Lyman O'Dell."

"You were married to that creep?" Russell looked at the lovely woman standing beside him and couldn't imagine her with the man who just left. He appeared to be fifteen years older and what most women would consider Hollywood handsome. But he knew far too well that pretty on the outside didn't necessarily mean pretty on the inside.

"He kind of caught me at a weak moment in my life. Long story, and I'm sure you're not interested in hearing about it."

Strangely and almost against his will, he did want to know. He needed to leave before he let himself get tangled up in someone else's problems, so he surprised himself when he said, "I started to ask you right before O'Dell got here. What's up with the lodge? I'm not an expert, but I know even off-season you need more than an old woman to help you. Where is everyone?"

"Don't you let Bella hear you call her old. We're a little down on workers at the moment, but I expect my main man back any day from his vacation and we have a couple that works here during the busy seasons. Are you looking for a job?"

Somehow, he knew that was coming and he'd walked right into it. He couldn't stay. He'd been here too long already. "No, but thanks for the offer. I need to be getting out of here. I appreciate the use of the cabin and the meals. You and your great-grandmother have been kind to me."

Maggie looked at him strangely and then shoved him causing all his weight to land on his bad leg. He grimaced in pain and bent over to grab his knee. "That's what I thought. I noticed the limp last night, and today your gimping about like a horse kicked you. Come to think of it, you did get kicked by a horse."

Russell straightened up and said, "What makes you say that?"

"I saw it happen last night. There's not much I miss around here. How many miles do you plan to travel walking like that? At least let Bella take a look at it. She's not only a witch," Maggie laughed. "She's a *curandera*."

Ah hell, he thought. He wasn't leaving anytime soon.

CHAPTER 3

Russell spent the rest of the morning arranging firewood in the yard according to the size of the logs. The day was bright and sunny, and he could smell the pine trees. It was slow going because his knee throbbed. He couldn't straighten out his leg, so his thigh was cramping.

He worked on creating a pile of kindling that the women could transport easily. It was a job that required two good legs, and at the moment, only one of his functioned correctly. He thought his knee would have improved some by now, but he was wrong.

When Magdalena called him in for lunch, he made his way toward the house, and although he tried his best to hide it, his prominent limp made that impossible. When he reached the table, he pulled out a chair and swung his body into it without putting any weight on his bum knee.

"This will not do at all," Bella said. "You must let me examine your leg."

"That's not necessary," he said.

"I'll be the judge of that," she said. "Drop your pants."

Russell felt his face flush with surprise. He was pretty sure blushing was something that had never happened to him before, and it made his embarrassment even worse. Before he could stop himself, he said, "No, ma'am, I will not," and he looked at Maggie to see if she had witnessed the whole humiliating exchange.

She was standing near the oven and peering inside. Her back was to them, and she did not turn around.

Bella made a sound that resembled a harrumph, stomped over to the kitchen counter, and pulled a pair of scissors out of the drawer. She steadily made her way across the room towards Russell, and he was sure she was going to hurt him. What the hell was he going to do? He couldn't manhandle an old woman.

When she reached his chair, she dropped to her knees and cut the leg of his jeans from hem to mid-thigh. He didn't dare move and could only hope her hand was steady enough not to cut his flesh.

He was so surprised, he simply sat there like a statue and let her have her way with him. She pulled open the slit in the jeans and put both hands on his knee, with one palm on each side. Then she used her thumb and forefinger to poke and prod and thoroughly examine him. It hurt like holy hell, but he clamped his mouth shut and was determined not to make a sound.

"Your knee is dislocated, and it has pulled all the muscles and tendons out of shape. Now your leg is sprained. I need to put your knee back in place. It's going to hurt. Want some whiskey first?"

"What? You're going to do what?" Maggie said. "Bella,

you can't do that. We need to take him to Angel Falls to the clinic."

"No," said Russell. "No clinic. Give me some whiskey and let's get it over with."

Later he would have trouble clearly remembering all the events that happened next. He knew he drank some whiskey, hobbled into the bedroom, and lay down on the bed. Then he drank more whiskey and let Bella stretch out his leg which lay in an unnatural position. He heard Magdalena asking questions.

"Are you sure it's not broken, Bella?"

"I'm sure. I've seen this happen to animals all the time. Always fixed it myself."

"Are you okay with this, Russell? Want me to stop her?"

He groaned and said, "Just do it."

Then, he felt her cool fingers on one side of his knee and her bony thumb on the other. She pushed on the kneecap with her thumb and pulled with her fingers, and after a few moments of excruciating pain, he heard a distinct pop, and suddenly the pain was gone.

∼

WHEN HE WOKE UP, he was still in that soft bed surrounded by lace and flowers and sweet-smelling bed linens. He saw Bella sitting in a rocking chair beside him. When he tried to sit up, she gently held him back.

"Go easy now. You might be dizzy at first."

He swung his legs over the side of the bed and saw an ice bag wrapped around his knee. "How long have I been asleep?"

"Not long," she said. "Maybe an hour. You passed out cold."

He smiled at her. "Thank you, Bella. You're a strong woman, and a wise one. You hurt me, but I think you helped me, too."

"Yes, I know I did," she said. "It will take a while for your sprain to heal, but your knee will be fine. The important thing is to stay off that leg until the soreness goes away."

He tried to stand up, but she held up her hand like a stop sign. "Maggie," she called, "get in here with those crutches."

Maggie came rushing in with a wooden crutch in each hand. "Here. Bella wants you to use these until your leg heals." She rested one on each side of him on the bed.

"I don't need those," he said. He tried to stand up and then realized that he had no strength in his leg and sat back down. "Well, maybe I do."

Maggie stood on one side of him and Bella on the other as they got him to his feet and slipped a crutch under each arm. Bella started to instruct him on their use, but he said that was not necessary. He had broken his ankle when he was a boy and remembered all too well how to use them.

Bella said she was going to make some coffee and would have a small meal ready for him in a few minutes. Then she left the room leaving him alone with Magdalena.

"I feel terrible about your knee," she said.

"What? Why? It's certainly not your fault." He remembered why he hadn't been paying attention to the horse and smiled. Maybe it was her fault, but he could not blame her for being beautiful.

"What are you smiling about?" she said.

To cover for his thoughts, he changed the subject. "I'm the one who should feel terrible. If I can't get around without crutches, I am going to be a huge burden for you. If you can think of anything I can do to help out around here, please tell me."

She thought for a moment, and then said, "How much do you know about computers?"

"I know a little."

"Well, my computer is quite old, and it's running really slow. Do you think you can fix it?"

"Depends. I'll be glad to take a look."

~

AFTER A DELICIOUS MEAL of pinto beans with pork and homemade flour tortillas, Russell made his way into the office and started working on the computer. He discovered after much trial and error that most likely Magdalena had accidentally downloaded a virus. He installed a free virus scanner from the Internet and ran it. The program found five issues and removed them. He did a test by running a video and audio file, and they ran at full speed.

He shut down the computer and slowly and clumsily made his way into the kitchen. As he walked past a long, oak table, he saw a series of old family photos. In one, Bella stood close to a tall, rugged-looking man, and he was sure that it was her husband.

Bella turned and wiped her hands on a kitchen towel when he entered the kitchen. "Better?" she asked.

He sat down in a chair at the table. "Yes," he said. "How long do you think I'll need these?" he indicated the crutches.

"As long as it takes. Do you want me to see what the cards say?"

"No thanks. Who is that in the photo with you?"

"What photo?"

"The one on the table in the office?"

"You trying to get into my business?"

He was confused. "What?"

"Why do you ask personal questions of me?"

He started to stand up and nearly fell. Knowing he was trapped, he sat back down.

"I'm sorry. I saw that photo, and I was curious. Never mind. Forget I asked."

"That's Reggie Morales." Her look softened. "I married him when I was seventeen years old. He was a good man. He knew how to take care of a woman."

At any other time, Russell would have taken her words at face value. But right now, he felt helpless and decided that she was shaming him. Her granddaughter was outside tending the horses, shoveling their dung, grooming and feeding them, and he was here sitting on his butt in the kitchen. He fell silent, and Bella went back to her dishes.

∼

HE COULDN'T WAIT to get out of there, so when Magdalena came into the house about an hour later, he asked her to take him back to his cabin. They rode on the ATV without saying much to each other, and she helped him into the small, comfortable living room.

"I'll be back in a little while with some things you will need," she said. "Are you going to take a nap? I don't want to wake you."

"Napping is not part of a normal day for me, so I would say no. Don't worry about it," he snapped.

"Well, okay then. I'll see you in about half an hour."

∼

TRUE TO HER WORD, she tapped on the door thirty minutes later. She had a paper bag in her hands that was overflowing with clothes. "I brought you some shaving cream and a razor, and some clean clothes that belonged to my grandfather. The pants will be a little short, but they will have to do until I can wash the ones you are wearing. Bella will sew up the slash she made in them, too. They will be almost as good as new."

She took the garments out of the bag and placed them on the kitchen table. "There's a bench in the shower, so I think you will be safe enough. The water is very hot, so be careful."

"You don't have to tell me that. I found that out the first time I used it."

"Well, I can wait for you in here, or I can leave and come back. It's up to you."

"I don't want to keep you from your chores," he said.

"They're all done. The rest of the afternoon is all mine to spend as I wish."

"You don't have to stay if you don't want to."

"Yes, I do. Your hair needs a good trim, and I've got some really sharp scissors." She held them up in her right hand.

The look on his face showed consternation. "Well … I …"

"Oh, come on now. Don't worry. I used to cut my grandfather's hair all the time."

∽

AFTER A HOT SHOWER, Russell dressed in the clothes she had brought for him. The shirt fit well, if a little snug through the chest, but she was right about the pants. They were a bit short although not enough to be comical. He would wear them until his own jeans were mended and washed. He toweled his hair dry and went back to the kitchen where she had a chair pulled out away from the table. He propped up his crutches and sat down awkwardly.

"Your grandfather was about my size, wasn't he?"

"Yes," she said while arranging a clean towel around his neck. "His name was Ernesto Morales, and I adored him."

"When did he pass?" he said. He was afraid to use the word *die* because it sounded so harsh.

"His heart gave out several months ago. Bella and I are learning to live without him, but our wounds are still fresh. He was only sixty-six-years-old."

"I'm so sorry," he said. "Losing someone you really love can leave a hole in your heart that will never heal." Then, because he feared that she would start asking questions about his life, he tried to change the mood.

"So, tell me about the business. Do you have lots of guests during the winter months?"

"We do," she said. "It's beautiful here, and the hot springs about two miles from here is a big attraction."

As she moved behind him and to the side of the chair her clean scent teased him. It wasn't perfume he inhaled, but something lighter and fresher. It must have been a body lotion or maybe her shampoo. Whatever it was, he could not remember a more pleasing fragrance.

She ran her fingers through his hair from front to back. He could feel her fingernails lightly scratch his scalp, and it tensed under her fingertips. Then she took a comb and combed his hair until all the tangles were out.

"Your hair is so thick," she said. "How do you like to wear it?"

"Longer in the back and shorter in the front." He reached up to feel his own hair, and their fingers touched.

"How short?"

"You can be the judge of that. Take off what you think needs to go, so I won't look so shaggy. I don't want to be mistaken for a bear."

As she worked and lifted his hair a section at a time and then combed it out and ran her fingers through it time and again, he felt her touch all the way to his toes and struggled not to groan with pleasure. It was fortunate that she had covered him with a big, loose towel. There was no way he could hide what her gentle way of raking her fingers through his hair was doing to him.

When she finished, she told him to go into the bathroom

and take a look in the mirror to see if he liked what she had done. He draped the towel in front of him as he left the room. A short time later he said in a loud voice, "The haircut is fine. I'm going to shave now if that's okay, and then we can go back to the house." He stayed in there an unusually long time.

∽

WHEN THEY GOT BACK to the house, Bella had dinner waiting for them. Maggie sat across from Russell and tried not to stare. Damn, if he didn't look good all showered, shaved, and trimmed up. Now that she could see the shape of his face and get a clear view of his eyes, she realized he was not the best-looking man she had ever seen, but his presence was compelling, and he had a ruggedness and vital power that attracted her.

He was nothing like her ex-husband who had the classic movie star looks and the stuck-up personality to go with it. No, nothing about Russell was polished. He had the craggy look of an unfinished sculpture.

His face was lean and chiseled, and it fit his six-foot-three frame. There was not an extra ounce of fat on his body that she could see. When she had covered his bare chest with the towel, she couldn't help but notice his muscles.

Tendrils of his thick brown hair fell onto his forehead and framed his face, and his piercing blue eyes reminded her of a winter lake. It would never do to get lost in those eyes. She thought she might freeze in place and be unable to look away. His face still had the memory of the dark stubble that he had recently shaved. She wondered how it would feel to run her fingers across the shadow of a beard on his cheeks. Would the whiskers be soft or scratchy?

"Maggie?" Bella said for the second time. "Did you hear me?"

"Sorry, what?"

"I asked if you wanted more chicken?"

"No, thank you, Bella, but it was simply delicious."

"Well, then. The meal is finished."

Maggie started clearing the dishes from the table and taking them to the kitchen counter.

"I can do these dishes, Maggie. You worked all day with the horses. You should rest now," said Bella.

"Thank you, Bella," Russell said. "That was a wonderful meal. I enjoyed every bite."

She smiled at him. "*De nada.*"

"Would you like to see if the computer is behaving better for you?" he asked Maggie.

"I would," she said and handed him his crutches.

He let her click around for a while to see if the computer was faster.

"It's really great," she said. "What did you do?"

"I ran a virus program and deleted some files that were slowing things down. No big deal."

"Well, thank you. A slow computer is about as frustrating as it can get. I like things that move fast. Patience is not one of my virtues." She clicked onto another screen, and the website for Cielo Verde showed up.

"Let me take a look at that," he said and took the mouse from her hand. As he clicked through the different pages on the screen, she moved away from the computer so he could sit down.

"Frankly, I think this website could use a makeover.

The fonts and the graphics are dated." He started to say that he could help her with that, but she interrupted him.

"Is that so? Well, if I wanted your opinion, I would have asked for it." Then she leaned over and hit the off button, and the screen faded to black.

What the hell? he thought. His mouth fell open in surprise as she stormed out of the room.

CHAPTER 4

On the ride from the main house to the cabin, Maggie could smell fall in the air. It was one of her favorite times of the year. Crisp but not yet cold. A light jacket was usually a good idea, but a coat wasn't necessary.

As she neared the small, neat cottage, she could see Russell sitting on the porch. He had his leg propped up on a stool but lowered it when he looked up and saw her. Men, she thought. They hated to admit any weakness even if it hurt like hell. She could relate in her own way. She had managed to stay afloat by not admitting defeat even though she knew the lodge was in serious financial trouble. She wasn't exactly ignoring her situation, but she could not bear to say it out loud.

"Morning," she called as she parked the ATV in the grassy driveway.

"Same to you," he said.

She noticed he didn't stand. Maybe he wasn't as much

of a gentleman as she thought, or perhaps he was trying not to fall on his face.

"What are you doing out here?"

He looked around as if he were taking a panoramic photo. "Oh, I'm keeping an eye on things."

"See anything interesting?"

"Nope."

She walked up the two wooden steps and slid gracefully into the wooden deck chair across from him. "Looking for anything particular?"

"Nope."

She chuckled. "Well, here's what I'm wondering."

He waited patiently looking at her with questioning eyes.

"If you did see something, what would you do about it?"

"Depends on if it were friend or foe."

"Do you know how to shoot a gun?"

He grinned and straightened his shoulders. "I've never had a need to use a weapon. I'm usually around civilized, peaceable people."

"Hang on," she said and bounded down the steps. Her boots kicked up dust as she made her way back to the vehicle. She opened a canvas pack attached to the handlebars and pulled out a pistol.

"Do you want me to teach you?"

"Now?"

"Sure. We'll head down the road about a mile. There's a dirt embankment where I've got some targets set up. It's safe to shoot there. No danger to any bystanders."

He thought for a minute and reached for his crutches. "Why not? Let's go."

"Okay, give me a few minutes. I'm going home to get the ammunition, the targets, and another gun. I'm coming back in Grandpa's' truck. It will be easier that way."

∼

A SHORT WHILE LATER, Maggie slowed the red, Ford pickup to a halt. After they got out, she told him that he could lean on the bed of the truck for balance. She didn't want to fill his head with too many directions at one time, but the basics were absolutely necessary.

"Okay, listen up. Always keep the gun pointed in a safe direction and away from people, especially me. Keep your finger off the trigger until you are ready to shoot. Rest your finger alongside the outside of the trigger guard."

She put the pistol in his hand, and he rested his arm on the frame of the truck bed. "Now, put your left hand under your right for support," she waited while he got into a shooting stance. "That's it. You've got the idea," she said. "Now, point the gun at the target."

"Like this?"

"Yes. This first time is to get the feel of the gun. Don't worry about hitting the target. When you put your finger on the trigger, squeeze it. Don't jerk it."

He stood there poised like a statue.

She waited a moment and then said, "What's the holdup?"

He laughed. "You are. You didn't say shoot."

"Okay, shoot."

He did. The shot rang out, and it kicked him backward. He tried to maintain his balance, but his leg was still too sore. He ended up on the ground with the gun in his hand pointed at the sky.

She thought he might be embarrassed, but he wasn't. "Well, damn, that little gun has a kick to it. Let me try that again."

The second time, he was ready for the recoil and held himself steady. Although he had the balance issue under control, his aim was far from accurate.

"It's a good thing I'm not at the OK Corral. I can't hit the target. It keeps going to the left."

"I think you are squeezing your support hand too tightly. Let's try it again," she said. She took her place behind him and leaned in close crushing her breasts to his back while adjusting the grip on his left hand.

"Do you think that what you're doing is helping me?"

"That's the idea," she said.

"Well, you're not. You're distracting the hell out of me."

She backed up unsure whether to be flattered or insulted.

After shooting three rounds, he was tired. "Let's call it a day," he said. "I think I've got the idea."

"You do," she said. "My grandfather would have said that you're a quick study."

"Was he your teacher?"

She smiled and busied herself picking up the discarded shell casings and cleaning up the area. "He was. He taught me to shoot, to fish, to hunt, and nearly everything I know about life."

"Sounds like a really great guy. I'm sorry for your loss, Magdalena."

She looked at him and her eyes filled with unbidden tears. "Thank you. I think I owe you an apology."

"You do? For what?"

"For the way I treated you yesterday in the office. I was rude, and you didn't deserve it. You were only trying to help me."

"Well, you're forgiven. But I still don't know what I did that made you so mad. Your website is fine. I was only trying to make it a little more modern."

"It's not that. I simply can't stand the idea that I am not living up to my grandfather's expectations. Cielo Verde was his creation and his dream, and I have turned it into a nightmare."

He put his hand on her shoulder. "Come on, now. It can't be as bad as all that."

She moved away and opened the driver's side door. "It's worse than you think. Get in and let's go. I need to get back."

∼

She drove slowly down the dusty, caliche roads on the way back to the house. There was nothing more to say about her troubles at the lodge without revealing her financial issues to Russell. He seemed like a really nice man, but he was, after all, a stranger.

"I want to stop at this water tank for a moment if you don't mind. There must be a problem with it because the runoff has slowed to a trickle and the horses aren't getting enough of a flow into their troughs."

They pulled up to a rusty water tank with an eight-foot ladder on the side. "Stay here," Maggie said as she opened the door and slid to the ground. She walked around the tank and then began to climb the steps. She wasn't up there long before she quickly descended and ran back to the truck.

"Got to get back and call the sheriff," she said in a breathless, raw voice. She started the truck, slammed it into gear, and tore off down the road.

~

RUSSELL REFUSED to leave Maggie and Bella alone, even though both of them told him they would be fine. All he knew was what he had heard her say to the sheriff on the phone.

"I'm not sure. I can't tell. All I could see was a shirt and a hat. Whoever it is was floating in the water."

She listened for a moment. "I don't know. I don't think I want to know. The only person who is still around is Marty, but I think he went to Santa Fe to see his cousin because the workload was so light around here."

Bella had retreated to the table and was turning her cards over one by one. She shook her head, and her gnarled hands trembled. "He's not in Santa Fe," she mumbled.

"What? What, Bella?" she turned to her grandmother and then back to the phone in her hand. "Let me know what you find, Sheriff. I'm really worried here."

Russell could see the tears in Bella's eyes, and it shook him to his core. This strong old woman did not often cry. He was sure of it. Who was Marty? He didn't dare ask. He busied himself in the kitchen while making tea and a strong pot of coffee for when the sheriff arrived. He thought he should locate the whiskey, too, but he had no idea where to look.

Magdalena had gone to the table to comfort her grandmother. "You don't know for sure, Bella. We have to wait and see." She rubbed small circles on her grandmother's back and clamped her trembling lips shut.

A loud knock on the door made all of them jump. The sheriff came in with a battered felt hat and a blue plaid shirt in his hands. Both were dripping wet. "Miz Bella," he said.

But he didn't need to say more. When she saw the clothing, Bella put both arms out in front of her on the table, rested her face on them, and sobbed.

Maggie looked like she was going to pass out. Russell quickly made his way to her side and guided her to the soft, worn sofa and sat beside her.

"I'm so sorry to say, that we found Marty Chavez's body in the water tank. Looks like he's been there a while. Can you tell me when you saw him last?"

Neither of the women answered his question. He looked to Russell for help, but he merely shrugged.

"Excuse me, sir. Have we met?" the Sheriff said.

"No, we haven't. I've only been here a couple of days, and I haven't been to town. And your name is?" he asked.

"I'm Sheriff Buckley. Are you kin to these ladies?"

Russell looked at Maggie who was crying softly and then back at Buckley. "No, I'm not related to them."

"What is your business here then?"

None of yours, he wanted to say, but instead replied, "I'm just passing through."

"What is your destination and where were you about a week ago?"

Russell shifted his position on the sofa.

"Buck," Magdalena said, "you have a lot of questions.

What I want is some answers. What happened to Marty? Did he fall in and drown?"

"I'm not sure yet, Maggie. We need to do some investigating first. We took him to the funeral home, so they can look him over."

"He didn't drown," Bella said from across the room. "He was a careful man. Been working for us for more than fifty years. He was family to us." She gulped hard as hot tears trickled down her cheeks.

"Bella's right," Maggie said. "He didn't drown. Somebody killed him."

CHAPTER 5

Roddy Eastman walked out the door of the hardware store and pulled his baseball cap over his curly, blond hair. The October sky was filled with early morning clouds that hung over the mountains awash with different hues of brilliant yellow, gold, and red leaves against the dark green pines.

Roddy was raised in Angel Falls and was in awe of the beauty he had taken for granted when growing up. Although he now lived less than two-hundred miles away in Albuquerque, the view there wasn't the same.

Angel Falls hadn't changed much in the last ten years. He passed Lucy's Diner and Smith's Grocery Store on his way to the post office. The store had recently been remodeled and added additional customer parking. He smelled the fresh baked goods coming from the diner and was tempted to stop in for a cup of coffee and one of Lucy's famous cinnamon rolls. Pulling the bill of his cap down, he greeted the elderly couple coming out the door.

"Morning, Mr. and Mrs. George."

"Why, Roddy Eastman. What in the world are you doing here? I thought you were some hotshot lawyer in Albuquerque."

Mr. George cleared his throat and said, "Don't you remember, Susan? Roddy's dad had that spell with his heart. I'll bet he's here to see about his dad and mom."

Roddy's deep voice rumbled when he said, "Yes, sir. That's correct. I'm helping out at the store while my dad's recuperating."

"Well, it's sure good to see you, young man, and awful nice of you to help out your daddy. You don't come around nearly enough," said Susan.

"That's what I hear, ma'am. It was nice seeing you both." Roddy tipped his hat again and walked on down the sidewalk.

The next greeting wasn't nearly as pleasant when the post office door swung open, and Eddie Buckley walked out. He was wearing the county sheriff's uniform that fit snuggly across his rounded stomach inching over his belt.

"Well, I'll be damned. If it isn't Little Roderick Eastman. Haven't seen you since you took off for that fancy college. Hope you're keeping your nose out of trouble these days."

"Hello, Buck. My dad said you'd been elected sheriff. I guess I should say congratulations," Roddy said with more enthusiasm than he felt.

"I can tell you're not too thrilled, but remember, this is my town now. You can't get away with all that stuff you did before."

"If you haven't noticed, Buck," Roddy looked down at the shorter man, "I haven't been a boy in years, and you were much too busy sleeping in your patrol car to cause me much worry."

The older man's eyes flashed with anger as he slapped the mail he had picked up against his thigh. "Like I said, you better watch it. I've still got my eye on you."

"You may have intimidated my friends and me when I was in my teens, but that won't work anymore. I'm not afraid of you."

"Friends, huh? Well, I hear one of your little friends is having hard times. Rumor has it she's about to lose that fancy place she's got."

"What are you talking about?"

"That little Spanish senorita you was always hanging with. Her granddaddy died, and she's been having all kinds of trouble out at her place. I guess you haven't heard. She found Marty Chavez floating in her water tank a couple of days ago. He's dead."

"You talking about Maggie Morales?"

"Yep, that's the gal."

"Marty's dead?"

"That's what I said. You deaf or something?"

Roddy took his hat off and ran his fingers through his hair. A lump had suddenly formed in his throat. Marty had been around forever. He'd been an integral part of Roddy's childhood, just as Maggie had been. "What happened? Heart attack?"

"Not sure, but I doubt it. Looks like somebody busted up his head real good. His body's been sent down to Santa Fe for an autopsy."

"You said Maggie's been having trouble. What kind of trouble?"

"Well, a couple of days ago she said someone let all the

horses out and before that one of the cabins got damaged. The mayor went out in person to check things out. She ran him off. I guess she's still got a burr up her butt since they divorced. He said she's got some drifter working out there. If you ask me, if anyone's doing any shenanigans it's him."

Roddy wanted to ask more questions but didn't want to spend another minute of the beautiful morning talking to Buck. He found it was always better to get information directly from the horse's mouth.

∼

MAGGIE WATCHED the silver Ford pickup turn off the highway and onto the road toward the lodge. She didn't recognize the vehicle but assumed it was a tourist that saw the lodge's sign. She only had a couple of cabins that were suitable for rental at the moment, but any paying customers would be welcome.

A tall, thin man shut the car door and walked toward Maggie. He was broad shouldered and wore a baseball cap that covered an abundance of blond hair. She noticed that big grin flash across his face, and she practically squealed in delight.

"Roddy," she exclaimed and ran into his arms. "Wow, it's great to see you. What are you doing here?"

"Here at your place or here in Angel Falls?"

"Both."

"Dad had heart bypass surgery and isn't supposed to go back to work for at least six weeks. When Mom said she was having a rough time keeping everything together at the store, I took a leave from the firm and came up to help."

"I'm so proud of you."

"Why? For being a good son."

"Well yes, of course, without saying. But, really for all you have accomplished. Getting your law degree and getting a plum job. I've kept tabs on you through your mom and dad. They showed me the newspaper article on that big case you handled last year."

Roddy took his cap off and frowned. "Geez, I'm sorry. It's not like I'm Perry Mason or anything."

"Come on up to the house. Bella would love to see you."

Roddy pulled her back when she started for the house. "Hey, Mags, I was sorry to hear about your granddad. I was in the middle of a trial and couldn't come to the funeral."

"We got your note and the flowers. It's okay. Bella will understand."

"And Marty. For heaven's sake, who would want to hurt Marty? He was about the gentlest soul around."

Fresh tears formed in Maggie's eyes and he pulled her closer. "I'm sorry, honey. Tell me. What's going on around here? I ran into the sheriff, or I guess what you'd call an excuse for a sheriff. How did that happen anyway?"

"Questions, questions, questions. Come on in the house and see Bella. We can talk about everything inside."

"Oh, before I forget." He handed her a small bundle he'd been carrying. "When I was in the post office, I took the liberty of getting your mail. I knew I'd be seeing you today after talking to Buck and wanted to save you a trip into town."

"How in the world did you get Lupe to give you my mail?" She looked up and watched him shrug and grin. "Okay, never mind. I forgot who I was talking to. Of course, Lupe gave you my mail. I'll bet she would have given you everything else she had too. I remember what a crush she had on you in high school."

～

Maggie placed a steaming bowl of potato soup and freshly made bread in front of Roddy and Russell. She was busy pouring coffee into cups and was oblivious to the hostile looks Russell was giving the other man.

"So, Mags, where is everybody? This place usually isn't humming this time of year, but it looks like a ghost town."

Maggie turned and set the cups down beside each bowl and took a seat next to Roddy. "Lyman O'Dell happened."

"He didn't get anything in the divorce. The place is legally Bella's isn't it?"

"It's not anything like that. You know we had no snow last winter and this summer we had the drought. Without any winter sports, the crowds don't come. Our revenue was way down, and then this summer the National Forest was closed. No campers to speak of."

"If you need a loan ..."

"Thanks, but we'll manage. Things have got to be better this year."

"How does Lyman fit into the picture?"

"His bank is building that Casino on the reservation. He's hired practically every worker from the age of seventeen through sixty, and he's paying top dollar. I can't compete with him. Everyone except Marty went to work for him. But let's not worry about that today. I would rather be Scarlett O'Hara and think about it tomorrow."

Roddy laughed and pulled Maggie in for a hug. "It's great to see you. You still my girl?"

"Always."

Russell looked back and forth between the pair. He couldn't figure out what was going on. Was this a serious relationship? If so, where had this guy been for the better part of a week? He didn't like the feelings bubbling up inside.

He looked back at Magdalena and noticed her chocolate brown eyes were locked on his face. "Are you all right?" she asked.

"Sure, why?"

"Roddy asked you a question."

"Oh, sorry, I guess my mind was somewhere else."

"I asked how you managed to end up at Cielo Verde?"

"Oh, just passing through." Russell was becoming increasingly uncomfortable and wanted to get up and leave, but for some reason, he didn't want to leave Magdalena with this man.

"I doubt that. This country is not exactly on the way to anything."

"I didn't have a particular destination in mind. I'm taking some time off."

"Time off from what?" Roddy insisted.

"Stop it, Roddy," Bella said abruptly. "Mr. Murphy will not cause us any harm. He is searching for his way. We are helping him find it. When you were a boy, I remember we helped you find yours."

Russell watched the other man's face turn red and then

smile at Bella. "You're right Bella. I'm sorry, Mr. Murphy. Maggie and Bella mean the world to me. I guess I'm a little overprotective. I should be glad someone is here to help look out for them."

"I don't need you or Russell looking after me," Maggie said. "I can take care of myself and Bella just fine."

Roddy smiled and winked at her. "I know you can, babe. You always have."

Russell watched Magdalena walk Roddy out to his truck. He noticed the way she leaned into him and the long hug that followed. He turned around to see Bella staring at him.

"She's a beautiful young woman. Any man would be glad to have her, don't you think, Mr. Murphy?"

"Yes, she is, and Roddy seems like a nice man."

"Oh, yes. He is a very nice man." The older woman laughed as if relishing a private joke. "I'm going to bed, but I'm sure I'll see you tomorrow."

~

MAGGIE WAVED goodbye to Roddy and returned to the kitchen. "After I check the mail Roddy brought, I'll give you a ride back to the cabin," Maggie said.

"I can walk. My knee's getting better every day. I should be ready to get out of your hair before much longer."

"No, wait, I'll take you …" She took a quick sharp breath.

"What is it?" Russell looked at the paper Magdalena held in her hand. "Bad news?"

She looked like she'd found out someone else had died.

Her expression was desolate. "Hey, what's going on?" Russell moved closer and touched her shoulder.

"Well, yes. It's the tax statement for the lodge that's due in January. I was expecting it. What I wasn't expecting was to get last year's bill, too." She sighed and threw the paper on the table. "It seems my grandfather neglected to pay it."

"Is it bad?"

"Oh, yeah, it's bad. Worse than bad. We made practically no money for the last two years. If we don't have a good season this year, I'm afraid I won't have to worry about Lyman buying this place. All he'll have to do is go to the tax office and pick it up for a song."

Russell pulled up a chair and sat close to her. "Do you have a plan?"

"No, do you?"

"Yes, I think I do."

CHAPTER 6

"Diversify? What do you mean?"

"Your grandfather's methods worked well for him for many years, but it's a brand-new world now, and all businesses have to reach out to new audiences if they want to stay competitive."

Maggie bristled a little. She didn't like it when anyone talked negatively about her grandfather. "You sound like you know what you're talking about. Who are you anyway?"

"I'm a guy that you and your great-grandmother have been kind to. I'd like to return the favor."

"Papa Ernesto did all right. We were doing fine until he got sick, and after that Cielo Verde had a couple of bad seasons."

"I mean no disrespect to him. The world moves fast, and it's hard to keep up no matter who you are. Since you can never predict the future, it's best to be prepared for whatever comes your way."

"How do you know so much?" Her dark eyebrows raised inquiringly.

He shrugged and gave her a lazy smile.

"You don't like to talk about yourself, do you?"

"No, I'm not very interesting."

"A man who appears out of nowhere from the mountains is not very interesting? I doubt that."

"Let's get back to what I was talking about. You have a beautiful home. I haven't seen much more than the great room and the kitchen. How many bedrooms are in the house?

"Why, you moving in?"

Russell laughed. It was a deep low rumble waiting to break free. This was the first time she'd heard him laugh, and Maggie would bet he hadn't done so in quite a while.

He slapped his hands on his thighs and stood up from the comfortable rocker in front of the main house. Maggie looked up into his piercing blue eyes and said, "Five. When my grandfather and his father added on to the house, they intended to have a lot of people under one roof. Unfortunately, that didn't happen. My great-uncle died in Vietnam, and my grandmother died giving birth to my mother."

She got up and took his hand. "Come on into the house. I'll show you around. With only Bella and me rattling around, all this space seems absurd."

Russell pulled his hand away as soon as they entered the house, but not fast enough so that Bella didn't notice. She gave Maggie one of her all-knowing smiles, which Maggie ignored and walked toward the main staircase.

The beautiful Spanish-style steps with wrought iron rails set on stone curved up to the second floor. Maggie turned when she noticed Russell had stopped halfway up. He seemed enthralled by the portrait of a woman whose face was awash from the hall lights. She had coal black hair and deep brown eyes surrounded by dark, full lashes. Her smile seemed intimate while remaining innocent.

"Is this …?"

"Yes, it's Bella. My great-grandfather had it painted for their first wedding anniversary. She's beautiful, isn't she?"

"You look a lot like her."

"Oh, I only wish. My grandmother was … well, I guess she still is a great beauty. She had a lot of suitors, but she only had eyes for my grandfather. She left her family at seventeen and followed him up here to what was a wilderness." She moved her hand around in a circle and said, "They made all of this. It's my legacy. I think it would break my heart if I ever had to sell it."

Maggie got a hint of something in Russell's face, but before she could identify it, he turned away. Who was this mystery man and why did she care? They walked down the hall, and she showed him the three upstairs bedrooms and adjoining baths.

"Which one is yours?"

"Bella and I have our rooms downstairs. I moved into my grandfather's room a couple of months ago. It took me that long to be able to go in without crying."

"You were close, then?"

"Oh, yes, very. Papa Ernesto was the only father I ever knew. Excuse me, but why the questions about the bedrooms?"

"As an option for making money in the off-season and even during a bad season would be to open a bed and breakfast. You have an ideal situation here."

She made a dismissing gesture. "I don't know. I've never thought about it. I'd have to cook and clean. As it is, I keep busy with all the other chores around here."

"You could employ a combination cook and housekeeper. Surely your ex hasn't hired all of those around town."

"If he thought I was in the market for someone like that, he'd snatch them up in a minute. I have a couple that works part-time for me during the busiest seasons, but I would need someone full-time. I'd like to hear more of your plans for diversifying. Let's talk some more about your ideas."

~

Bella had retired to her room to rest, and Russell went back to his cabin. Maggie rubbed her brow as she looked at all the suggestions he had written on the piece of paper lying on her desk. Where had he come up with all these ideas? The man looked like a Roman Gladiator but had the mind of a Warren Buffett.

Her phone rang, and she groaned when she saw Lyman's name on the screen. "Oh hell, what does he want now?" she muttered.

"Hello, Lyman."

"Maggie, sweetheart, I'm calling to offer my condolences. I heard about Marty Chavez."

"Why? You never liked the man because he could see right through you."

"I'll admit we didn't hit it off, but he was important to you, and I know how you must be hurting."

Maggie wanted to tell him he had no idea what she

was feeling, and she didn't want his sympathy but knew her words would be wasted. She was convinced Lyman O'Dell did not have a soul. "Thank you. If there isn't anything else, I'm a little busy to chat."

"Well, yes, there is this one thing. I also heard about your tax problem. I'd be—"

"How the hell do you know anything about my taxes? Are you reading my mail now?"

"As I said before, I'm the mayor. People tell me things."

"If someone in the county office is telling you things about me, I'll make sure my attorney sues his ass and yours too." She could hear him making the clucking noise with his tongue that she hated and gritted her teeth.

"Sweetheart, because of your grief over your friend, I'm not going to take anything you're saying personally, and I would like to let bygones be bygones. I'll raise my offer another twenty thousand dollars. That's more than you will get from anybody else. Take the money. Move Bella into town into a lovely little cottage."

Maggie's temper exploded, and she pounded the phone on her desk. "You are a swine, Lyman O'Dell, without any sense of honor. No scruples, no conscience. I wouldn't put it past you to have done something to Marty yourself. You'll never get my home. Do you hear me? Never." She pushed the red end button and sent her phone flying across the room.

∽

OCTOBER NIGHTS WERE COLD. Even if the days were mild, as soon as the sun began its descent, the night air would make even the most diehard mountain man shiver. He saw Maggie, covered with a blanket, seated in front of the fire pit. She tilted up a bottle and took a drink. Russell couldn't tell what she was drinking, but as he watched her sway back and forth to non-existent music, he figured it wasn't lemonade.

His leg was well enough now that he could move on. He'd come to tell Magdalena he'd be leaving in the morning. It was time. Earlier, while shaving and combing his hair, he realized that he shouldn't get more involved in Maggie's and Bella's lives. He and Maggie had brainstormed lots of ideas for turning the lodge around. She'd be okay, he told himself. Wouldn't she?

He looked down at the clean shirt and jeans he was wearing. In the last few weeks, he'd gained some weight and no longer looked like a starved refugee. He felt good for the first time in months. Yes, it was time to move on. He was beginning to care way too much.

"Magdalena?" he spoke softly.

She turned, and the blanket slipped showing the down-filled coat zipped up to her neck."

He chuckled and said, "You look like Nanook."

"Who?"

"Some guy who lived in the Arctic. They made a movie about him years ago."

"Oh," she said and took a long gulp from the bottle while pulling the blanket back up to her neck. "Nanook, that's cute."

And so are you, he wanted to say but sat down on one of the chairs facing her instead and warmed his hands over the fire. "What are you drinking?"

"Chateau Brane Cantenac. I believe it costs about four hundred dollars a bottle. I took it and all the other fine, expensive wines I could cram in my car when I left the cheating bastard."

"By cheating bastard, I assume you are referring to Lyman."

"Yep, they are one and the same." She waved the bottle over her head and smiled across the fire at Russell. "Would you like a drink?"

The reflection of the fire danced across her face showing her dark, seductive eyes surrounded by her wild, untamed hair. She was the most beautiful thing he'd ever seen. "What's the matter? What are you doing out here?"

She got up and let the blanket fall to the ground as she turned around in circles while reaching her arms toward the sky. "Isn't it the most gorgeous thing you've ever seen?"

Russell gulped, his voice raspy as he said, "Yes, gorgeous," never taking his eyes off her.

"You can see all the stars. They seem to go on forever and ever. Do you think they ever end?"

Russell walked around the fire and reached for the bottle. Surprisingly, she let it go. It was nearly empty, and he was a little surprised she was still standing. "Tell me what's going on?"

She plopped back into her chair and sighed. "I'm worn out, Russ. I don't know how much longer I can fight. Lyman called today. Somehow, he knows about the back taxes. He's such a pig. He thinks he's going to win. I'd rather burn this place to the ground than give it to him."

"How did you end up with a guy like him anyway?" He pulled his chair close to hers, their knees touching.

"I was in college in Colorado majoring in accounting. I knew I was never going to leave this place, but I wanted to be able to contribute and make everyone's life a little easier. When I got the call, she assured me that she was going to be okay."

"Who?" he said. His voice was gentle.

"My mother. She had leukemia, and she was dying. Of course, I came home at the end of the semester and got a job in the mayor's office."

"You went to work for Lyman?"

"Well, no, not at first. I went to work for the incumbent mayor, but Lyman with his brilliant smile and Hollywood looks swept the next election. Being the mayor is a part-time position, and Lyman needed help in the beginning since being president of one of the banks in town keeps him busy."

Russell kept his gaze on her, and his eyes reflected his interest.

"He decided to keep me on since I knew the routine and how to run the office. I always thought it was because I was doing a good job. In reality, it was because I was the heir to Cielo Verde."

"Magdalena, you're a bright, accomplished woman. I'm sure that wasn't the reason."

She exhaled and blew the hair out of her eyes. "I was young and dumb. When Mama died, I was devastated, and that's when he went in for the kill. Bella told me not to do it. She showed me the cards, and I drew the seven of swords that showed deception and betrayal, but I was young and sure that I was in love. I foolishly ignored her advice and my grandfather's disapproval."

Russell wanted to take her in his arms and comfort her, but he knew he couldn't do it. He was sure if he ever touched her, he would never want to let her go.

"When Lyman found out I didn't own any part of the lodge, he got angry. The property belongs solely to Bella, and then when she passed, it was to go to Papa Ernesto. By marrying me, Lyman really got nothing except a used Chevy Tahoe and my college debt."

"Go on." He touched her elbow lightly, urging yet protective.

Her voice sounded tired. "Of course Lyman didn't know that when he arranged for me to find one of his secretaries and him in our bed. I guess he figured he could divorce me and get half of my share of the property. Needless to say, he was quite upset."

She shifted in her chair and reached for the bottle. "I miss my mother and my grandfather so much," she said as tears streamed down her face. "I'm trying to be brave, but I'm sure I'm going to let Bella and Papa Ernesto down. Lyman's going to win."

As tears blinded her eyes and choked her voice, Russell did the one thing he didn't want to do. He pulled her into his arms and settled her on his lap against him. He looked up at the brilliant stars and then down at the dark-haired woman. His heart swelled with a feeling he had thought long since dead.

CHAPTER 7

With her heart thumping erratically in her chest, Maggie ran out of her room and straight into Bella's waiting arms.

"Mija, what is it? Shh ... shh ... it's okay. Everything is okay. Bella is here. Nightmare?"

"Yes, no, I don't know. Look at me. Last night I cried like a baby and now this morning I'm a total mess."

"What happened last night with Russell?"

"How did you ...? Oh, never mind. He was kind and listened while I made a complete fool of myself with the help of a bottle of expensive wine. I should have sold it to pay some bills instead of wasting it on my pity party."

"Why would you have a pity party?"

"Papa Ernesto didn't pay the taxes at all last year, and now this year's taxes are due. We don't have the money to pay them. We may have to sell the property to keep the county from taking the land." Maggie saw the concern in her grandmother's face. "I didn't tell you because I didn't want you to worry and now look what I've done."

The worry immediately vanished from the old woman's face, and confidence took its place. "Then we must come up with a way to keep the wolf at bay, yes?"

"Well, yes. Russell had several suggestions but ..."

"It's good then, that he is going to stay. You are friends."

"You talk in riddles Bella. What do you know?"

"Very little, since you won't let me read you, and that man keeps his distance from me since I got a glimpse. But I do know that when all his secrets come tumbling down, he will need you. Now, what has happened this morning? Another dream?"

"Yes, it was Emma. She was in the meadow like she always is. She was smiling and happy, but then she started to cry. It was horrible. She was devastated, and I couldn't help her. She was begging me to come to her, and I couldn't do anything. What does it mean?"

"We can look and try to see," Bella said taking out a crocheted bag that contained her cards.

"I'm going crazy, Bella. I can't sleep. Every night. Some nights are better than others, but last night was scary. I don't understand why I am having these dreams."

"What did you do last night that was different before you went to sleep?"

"Like I said, I got really drunk and said a bunch of stuff, and then, I started crying and Russell pulled me into his arms. I'm pretty sure he was coming to tell me he was leaving, but he didn't since I completely fell apart. His limp is nearly gone now, and I don't think I want him to go. I felt so ...."

"Safe?"

"Yes, for the first time in a long time, but I don't know why. I'm certainly not afraid of Lyman."

Bella spread the cards across the table and turned several over. "Let's see what the tarot will tell us."

Maggie watched Bella's facial expressions but knew she would see no reaction. Bella's face always remained passive when she did a reading. As a young child while growing up with her great-grandmother, Maggie thought the woman was magical. When Maggie became a teenager, she gave in to peer pressure and complained to her mother that what Bella did was creepy. Of course, her perspective changed as she became an adult, and now she took what Bella could do in stride. Maggie often heard things she didn't want to know, but Bella told her anyway.

"There has been deceit and betrayal," Bella said when she flipped the first card over.

"Well, that's no big surprise. I know Lyman is a cheat and a liar and is trying to steal our land."

Bella lightly touched Maggie's face and smiled sadly. "Why do you think this refers only to your past? Maybe there is something in your dreams from someone else's past. Perhaps you are meant to help someone. Maybe these dreams are meant for that."

Maggie thought about the statement and tried to determine why a little girl would be in her past. She had no children. Had never really been around children. How could she help a child she'd never met? She didn't even have friends who had young children.

When Bella turned the next card over, Maggie recognized the woman with the sword. She'd seen the card before in other readings. Bella pointed to it and said,

"This has always been you, mija. Powerful and confident. Don't let O'Dell take that from you. You have suffered great losses as I have, but it has only made you stronger. You will know what to do when the time comes, and you will be strong for the ones you love.

Your circle will widen. There will be room to love and trust again. See? This card tells me there will be a child in your future. Don't run away from it if this is what you desire."

As Bella continued the reading, Maggie felt torn between the promise of new beginnings and the desire to keep things the way they had always been. When the reading was over, she still didn't know why a young girl visited her dreams nightly, but she now saw her dream as a puzzle she needed to solve rather than something to fear.

Bella chuckled and said, "You know the cards only tell you what was and what could be. You have free will, and your future is of your making. I see good things for you, but there will be obstacles and trials before you reach your goal. Be strong. Trust yourself and trust those around you that you love."

But, Maggie thought, *I don't love anyone but Bella, do I?*

∼

WHEN MAGGIE LEFT the room to get dressed for the day, Bella took the opportunity to drive to Russell's cabin. When he heard the roar of the ATV engine, Russell walked out onto the porch. He felt a little apprehensive after last night. He didn't know how to act and was sure he should never have held Magdalena in his arms. He stopped short when he saw Bella.

"Good morning, Mrs. Morales. I thought you were Magdalena."

"Sorry to disappoint. Maggie slept late this morning. I think you already know something about that."

"Yes, did she tell you what happened?"

"No, did something happen that I should know about?"

Russell frowned, scratched his head and said, "Are you yanking my chain, ma'am?"

"Pardon?" Bella said smiling.

"It means teasing, but you know that don't you?"

"Please call me Bella, and yes I am teasing you. Maggie told me she had too much to drink and poured her heart out to you. Knowing her, she'll try to avoid you today. She's probably a little embarrassed."

"There's no need for her to be. I know I've felt the same way lots of times."

"I'm thankful that you changed your mind," Bella said getting down from the vehicle. Her long hair was pulled back in a soft bun and tucked under a sparkly silver cap. She wore simple denim jeans and a flannel shirt and boots. Russell thought she didn't look like any great-granny he'd ever met before.

Puzzled he said, "What did I change my mind about?"

"You had decided to leave today. Now, I see that you have changed your mind. I want you to know that is the right decision, but that's not the reason I came to see you." Bella reached for his hand, and Russell immediately stepped back.

"A cautious man, aren't you?" She laughed and winked. "That's not the reason I came to see you either. I need you to run a couple of errands for me in town. Here are the keys to the truck and the list for the hardware store. It's time you got out and about, saw the town, and met some people since you're not going anywhere anytime soon."

She climbed back on the ATV and turned it around. Then, she turned and yelled, "Oh, and please get the mail."

Russell stood there shaking his head and wondering what the hell had just happened. He felt sure he'd been manipulated, but he wasn't sure why.

∽

IT HAD BEEN a while since Russell had driven a truck or any other vehicle. When he'd decided to go off the grid, he'd barely given a thought to transportation and had relied on his two feet to get around for the better part of a year.

He'd never been to Angel Falls and wasn't sure what to expect. He was pleasantly surprised to see a small but prosperous community. His first stop was the post office. A quick in and out since Bella had given him the key to the box. Next, he visited the hardware store. He'd taken a quick glance at the list but had no idea why Bella would need the items listed. He shrugged. It wasn't any of his business.

An attractive older woman was standing behind the counter finishing up a sale to a weathered man who wore overalls, a long sleeve thermal shirt, and a stained cowboy hat. Russell nodded and waited his turn.

"Yes, sir," the woman said. "What can I help you with?"

Russell handed her the list and grimaced. "It's kinda long. If you will point me in the right direction, I can get the stuff."

"Nonsense, that's our job." The woman picked up a two-way radio and said, "Roddy can I get some help up front."

Oh crap, Russell thought as Roddy Eastman came out the door from the backroom. *This must be the store where the golden boy is helping his folks out. Thanks a lot, Bella*, Russell thought.

"Hey, Russell," Roddy said grinning from ear to ear. "What's up?"

"You know each other?" the woman said.

"Yep, Russell is Maggie's latest project."

"Why, Roderick Eastman, you apologize this instant." She turned to Russell and said, "My son lost his manners when he went off to school. I'm sure they'll come back to him anytime now. I'm Wanda Eastman, Roddy's mother."

"Nice to meet you, ma'am. I'm Russell Murphy, and Roddy is correct. Maggie and Bella have been very kind to a stranger. I wasn't aware that Maggie had other projects."

"Oh yeah, when we were in school together, she was always bringing something home. Usually, the poor critter was half dead. You're a step up though. You don't look like you're any worse for wear."

Jerk, Russell thought. Roddy was practically hanging all over Maggie at dinner the other night. Exactly what was going on between the two and why should he care anyway?

"Hey, man, I'm kidding," Roddy said. "What do you need?"

Wanda handed the list to Roddy and moved to help another waiting customer.

"Well, let's go see what Maggie wants," Roddy said.

"Not Maggie."

"Oh?"

"No, Bella gave me the list this morning."

"Hmm, okay. Let's go see what we got." Roddy came out from behind the counter and walked down one of the aisles. Russell hesitated and then followed close behind the other man.

"What are you planning to do with all this stuff?"

"I have no idea. I guess some painting. Sounds like you've known Maggie for a long time."

"Oh, yeah. We go way back to kindergarten. In a town this small, there aren't that many students, so we were always together."

I'll bet you were, Russell thought.

"She was a real looker in high school. Popular too. We had some really great times."

Russell looked at Roddy again and wanted to ask if they were ever lovers, but he wasn't sure he wanted to hear the answer.

After all of the items were collected, Russell walked with Roddy back to the counter. Roddy gave his mother a generous smile and slapped Russell on the back. "I told Russell here, Maggie and I have been together since grade school. You can ask Mom, we practically lived at each other's homes."

Russell couldn't wait to get out of the store. He didn't know why he was angry. If he didn't know better, he'd think he was jealous, but that was ridiculous. He barely knew Magdalena.

"What was that all about?" Wanda asked her son as soon as Russell closed the front door.

"When I was out at Mag's place for supper the other night, I could see the sparks flying back and forth between the two of them. I was fanning the flames, Mom, just fanning the flames."

CHAPTER 8

Russell saw the flashing sign for Lucy's Café and decided he needed a cup of coffee and a few minutes to gather his thoughts before he drove back to the lodge. His mind was racing all over the place, and for the first time in a long time, he felt a small piece of contentment. He knew he didn't deserve happiness, but some of the dark fog he'd existed in for months had lifted because of Magdalena and Bella.

Deep in thought, Russell watched the coffee swirl around as he gently moved his cup between his hands. A shadow fell across the table, and he raised his eyes to see Lyman O'Dell's fake smile. Russell guessed since Lyman was a politician, it was permanently frozen that way.

"Murphy, isn't it? Mind if I take a seat?"

Russell didn't answer and stared coldly at the other man.

"I see you're still around. I thought you'd have taken off by now, but then again, Maggie may have given you a pretty good offer to stay." His tone was insulting and meant to imply that Maggie was trading sex for labor. Russell didn't rise to the bait and continued to drink his coffee.

"I certainly can't offer you what she can, but if you are looking for a high-paying job, I could always use a big guy like you." Lyman took a card out of his wallet and slid it across the table. "It would be nice having someone on the payroll that was, you know, close to Maggie."

Lyman tapped his fingers on the table and cleared his throat. "You don't talk much do you?" Lyman said.

Russell slowly moved only his eyes to send a piercing glare in Lyman's direction.

"Now that you're all cleaned up, I almost didn't recognize you. Speaking of, have we met before that day out at Maggie's place? You look familiar," Lyman said.

Russell slowly moved his coffee to his right and said, "We haven't met. If we had, I'd still be trying to get the crap off my shoe."

Lyman opened his mouth to object, but before he could, Russell grabbed the weasel's expensive red tie and knotted it in his fist. "If you ever disparage Magdalena's good name in my presence again, you will need to replace those shiny, capped teeth because they'll be scattered all over the floor."

He released Lyman, laid a five-dollar bill on the table, and calmly walked out the door.

∼

MAGGIE THOUGHT SEEING Russell again after the night she'd cried in his arms would be awkward, but to her surprise, it wasn't. Russell hadn't mentioned it, and the past couple of days passed quickly. Bella had outdone herself with the building materials she'd requested. She explained that since they were going to have a man around to help for a while, they needed to put him to good use. The only problem was, Russell had never pounded a nail or painted a wall in his life.

Fortunately, Maggie had done both. Papa Ernesto had been an excellent teacher, and Maggie had followed him around since she could walk. He taught her to frame a wall, hang, tape, and float drywall, and paint like Picasso. She could also ride a horse, shoot and dress a deer, and grill a darn good T-bone steak.

Russell was a quick study and picked up the skills necessary to make any construction foreman proud. They'd been working on one of the cabins that had been vandalized and needed a multitude of repairs. Maggie made a pot of coffee and poured a cup for each of them.

"Take a break. You've been at it all morning," she said. "You take it black, right?"

Russell climbed down from the ladder and ran his fingers over his hair brushing off the dried paint chips. "Yes, thanks." Taking the coffee Maggie offered, he pulled out one of the kitchen chairs that still had four legs and sat.

Maggie took a seat on the dusty floor leaning her back against the wall. "I'm wondering how is it that a man your age, what is it thirty, thirty-five doesn't know how to use a hammer?"

"Yeah."

"Yeah, what?"

"Closer to thirty-five."

"I thought only women were afraid to tell their age."

His lips turned up in a half smile, and he said, "I'll be thirty-four next June."

"And the rest of the question?"

"I never learned. Never had the time or the need to fix up a house, and you're exaggerating a little. I never said I didn't know how to use a hammer."

"Hmm. Me, I've been a tomboy all my life. I guess I had more guy friends than girls."

"Yeah, Roddy kind of mentioned that."

"When did you see Roddy?" She sucked her lip and then said, "Oh, sure. At the store."

"I met his mother, too. Nice woman. I guess you were a fixture around their house when you and Roddy were an item."

"Who told you that? Wanda?"

"No, Roddy."

Maggie got up from the floor, moved closer to Russell, and slammed her cup down spilling coffee on the table. "Roddy told you that he and I were an *item*? He said those exact words?"

"Well, no," Russell said and wiped the puddle of coffee with his sleeve. "Not exactly those words. He said that you were close, and you were around all of the time, and …"

Maggie burst out laughing. "And, since I'm a woman and he's a man then we must have been in each other's pants." The statement hung in the air, and it was several seconds before Russell responded.

"I take it you and Roddy were …"

"Friends. Just friends. I'm going to snatch him bald for giving you any other impression."

"I guess that's my fault. I pretty much assumed …"

"And you know what happens when you assume?"

"Yeah, yeah, I know. It makes an ass out of you and me. I'm sorry."

"Where are you from, Mr. Murphy?"

"New Mexico."

Maggie picked her coffee cup off the table and started for the door. She was angry and didn't care if he knew it. "I guess we're back to day one when you walked off the mountain. I thought we had become friends. Guess I was wrong. See you later, Russ."

The silence was uncomfortable until she touched the door handle. Then, she heard him say, "Tucumcari. I grew up in Tucumcari."

She turned around and chuckled. "Gosh, I'm really sorry."

His lip curled up and turned into a wide grin. "Yeah, me too."

She waited for him to continue, and when he didn't, she sighed and said, "And?"

"It was only my father and me for several years until he remarried."

"What happened to your mother?"

"Don't know. One day she was there and the next she wasn't. I was too young to remember much."

"That happened to me too. Not my mother, my father. I don't even have his last name. I think he's someplace out in California. That's where my mom met him. She aspired to be an actress, but that didn't exactly work out the way she planned. When he took off after I was born, she came back home."

"Did you ever look for him?"

"No, I never wanted to. I had plenty of love from Bella, Papa Ernesto, and my mom. How about you?"

"Nah, she didn't want me. I didn't want her. My stepmother was okay. She mostly raised me. I have a stepbrother, but he was just a baby when they got married. We weren't particularly close. My dad drank a lot, and I managed not to be home most of the time. I got out as fast as I could."

"How'd you do that?" Maggie turned around when she heard scratching and a pitiful whine at the door. She opened it, and a dirty exuberant Boney ran wiggling and jumping into the room. "Whoa, boy, where have you been? Chasing rabbits?"

The dog circled three times and plopped down beside Russ.

"My dog seems to like you more than me these days," Maggie said.

"It might be the bacon I sneak him every morning." Russ stroked the dog under his chin and was rewarded with a thumping tail. "Roddy said you are good at taking in strays. Is that why you let a virtual stranger take up residence?"

"I'm not the best judge of character, but Bella, you know, has a sixth sense about such things. She had Lyman all figured out the first time she met him. If she wasn't concerned that you were a homeless serial killer, then I certainly wasn't."

"I'm not homeless."

"Are you a serial killer then?"

Something flashed in Russell's eyes, but he didn't make any further comment.

"Before Boney so rudely interrupted us, you were telling me how you got out of Tucumcari."

"I went to college as far away from there as I could get."

Maggie looked at Russell. He was a big, rough-looking man, and being a college graduate was the last thing she would have expected. "Football scholarship?"

"No."

"Wrestling? Baseball?"

"No and no. Why would you assume I'm all brawn and no brains? I'm done talking about me. I'm going to get back to work now."

"Wait, I have one more question. You got an academic scholarship?"

"Yep, to MIT." He stopped, looked at her and grinned. "Close your mouth, Magdalena or flies will get in it."

CHAPTER 9

Lyman O'Dell left the bar and crossed the lot where he had parked the Land Rover. He slid into the driver's seat, adjusted the seat belt, and put his hand on the ignition button. Before he could push it, he heard a noise from the back seat but didn't have time to react before a large, beefy hand clamped across his mouth and pressed his head back against the seat.

"Umm, wait," he moaned while trying to talk.

"Shut your mouth and do what I say," a deep, male voice said. "Start this car and drive it out of town about a mile or two. We need to have a talk."

Lyman assumed the man had a gun, so he didn't attempt to be a hero and followed instructions.

"Pull over here and stop," the man said. "Turn the car off and hand me the key fob."

Lyman followed his orders and was rewarded with a blindfold tied tightly around his eyes.

"Isn't this a little dramatic?" he asked. His voice dripped with sarcasm.

"Shut the hell up," the voice said. "Boss said you weren't to get a look at me while I set you straight."

Lyman swallowed and tried to regulate his breathing. With the mention of the boss, he knew who this messenger was, and he was pretty sure he knew the message as well.

"Here's what you need to know. Boss says you missed your last two payments, and so far, you've done nothing to get your ex-wife to sign over her land. You're not holding up your end of the deal, and the boss is getting tired of waiting."

"Listen, I said I would try to get Magdalena to sell her land. Try is the operative word here. I never said I was sure I could pull it off," Lyman said. "I've done everything I know how to do, but nothing is working out like I thought it would."

"We kinda figured you'd bust your balls to get that money you were promised. I'd of found a way to pull it off if it were me. Boss said he was going to cancel your Vegas debts and give you a hundred K as well. Nobody gets a deal like that. He must want that land awful bad."

"He does. He has a master plan to build townhomes and a golf course on it and make millions. A piddling hundred thousand is peanuts to him." Lyman could not hide his sarcasm.

"Well, here's the deal. The old man who was going to squeal to the state police ended up floating in a water tank, and the many attempts at making life difficult for your ex haven't worked. Now it's up to you. If you don't figure out something pretty quick, Boss is going to clear the way himself, if you know what I mean. No more chances for the little lady, and your debts are going to land you in a six-foot hole."

~

MAGGIE SURPRISED herself by agreeing to have dinner in town with Russell. She took the time to wash her hair, apply a spritz of cologne, and dress in slim black jeans and a bright turquoise blouse. She left the two top buttons open so that if she turned a certain way, a hint of her smooth, olive-skinned cleavage peeked out.

When he knocked on her door, excitement added shine to her eyes and a rosy glow to her cheeks. "Come in, Russell. I'm sure Bella would like to say hello before we leave."

Bella was seated in her comfortable, white, wing-backed chair near the fire. Thanks to Russell, it was piled with logs and burning brightly. It was warm enough that Bella's lap robe still lay neatly folded in the basket beside her.

"You look very handsome tonight, Russell. I like the look of a man in jeans and a vest. My Reggie had a cowhide vest that he wore on special occasions. He was a fine figure of a man. I wish you could have known him."

Russell seemed embarrassed with the compliment and mumbled his thanks.

"Well, we should go," Maggie said. "There won't be anything left of the prime rib they cook on Saturday night. We might have to settle for a T-bone."

She put on a fur-lined coat, and Russell opened the door and let her lead the way. She surprised him by tossing him the keys to the truck. He helped her inside, and then slid into the driver's seat and adjusted the mirror.

"You know how to drive a stick shift?"

His brow pulled into an affronted frown. "You're kidding, right?"

"Why would I be? I don't know you at all. You could be a city-slicker who calls a cab when he wants to go somewhere."

"And if I were? Is that something to be ashamed of?" He turned the key in the ignition, and after sputtering a bit, the engine started. The smell of gasoline was strong in the cab of the truck. "Besides, I drove this thing to town a few days ago. By the way, this old truck could use a tune-up. One of these days it's not going to start."

"And if I pay you, can you do it?" she said.

He rolled down his window to let the fresh air dissipate some of the fumes. Amusement flickered in the eyes that met hers. "Now that is a sneaky way to get more information about me."

"Well, can you?"

"Actually, no. Not a chance. I never worked on a car in my life except to change the oil. It doesn't appeal to me. But if you give me a manual, I guess I could figure it out." He grinned at her. "How about you? Are you mechanically inclined?"

"Not at all. That's why many things are broken and in need of repair at the lodge. Papa Ernesto always took care of all that." Her eyes misted and the color drained from her face.

"Tell you what," he said and took his eyes off the road to look at her, "let's stop interrogating each other and have a good meal and take a break from all serious conversation tonight. Deal?"

The beginning of a smile tipped the corners of her mouth. "Deal."

Maggie was quiet until after they ordered, and she squirmed in her seat while trying to keep from opening her mouth, but she couldn't stay silent. "I know we said no interrogations, but I've got to say this, Russ. I haven't been thinking of anything else since you told me. You frigging went to MIT. Only brainiacs get into MIT, and you got a scholarship there. And now you're homeless? What gives with that?"

Russell lifted the glass to his lips and took a sip of water. He put it down slowly and looked across the table at her. Maggie wasn't sure what he was thinking. Was he angry? Disappointed? She hadn't meant to upset him.

"I told you I'm not homeless, and I'm not destitute. I invited you to dinner, and I have the money to pay for it. My life is a little bit complicated, and I'm not ready to talk about it right now."

"I'm sorry, I hope I haven't ruined the evening. I've never met anyone like you before, Russ. You're a puzzle, and I like to solve puzzles."

His eyes were gentle and understanding "You haven't ruined anything. I'm looking forward to a great meal and maybe a piece of the famous pecan pie I saw on the menu."

∼

BELLA CLEANED her face and applied the rich olive oil and lavender cream she had used for years. Her long silver hair was braided and tucked up on her head for the night. She folded her clothes and slipped on her soft, cotton nightgown and crawled into the bed between clean, fragrant sheets. It had been a long day, and she was tired. After saying her prayers and goodnights to everyone she loved who had already departed this earth, she closed her eyes and fell into a deep sleep.

She could hear Boney barking, and it sounded like he was miles away. Was that part of her dream? She opened her eyes and let them adjust to the darkness and then made her way toward the sound of his rapid, frantic yelps. She pulled on a coat, grabbed the shotgun from the rack on the wall, opened the door, and followed the dog out.

Boney took off in a dead run. Bella could see at least two men near the barn. Then she smelled gasoline, and she knew what they were doing.

She fired the gun into the air. "Stop right there," she demanded. "Whoever you are, you have no right to be here on my land. I swear I'll shoot you dead if you don't get out of here."

She could see them pouring gasoline all around the hay bales outside the barn, but before she could take aim, one of the thugs knocked her to the ground, took the gun from her hands, and slammed it across her face and head. He threw the shotgun into the dirt and weeds.

Boney, still barking frantically, leaped up and clamped his jaws onto the arm of the man who stood above Bella. The man screamed in pain and tried to sling the dog off of himself. Finally, a shot rang out, and Boney fell to the ground beside Bella.

The fire had taken hold now, and the men grabbed the gas cans and jumped into the truck.

"Wait, what about the old woman?"

"What about her? Let's get the hell out of here."

∽

THE SCENE that Maggie and Russ saw as they topped the hill and started down the road to the lodge was one out of a horror novel. Smoke and flames billowed from the barn.

Russ slammed on the brakes, jumped out of the truck, and raced to the side of the house to turn on the water hose. He began dousing the base of the flames with water while calling out to Maggie who had run into the house and then back out again.

"Was she in there?" he yelled. "Did you find her?"

"No," Maggie said as she rigidly held back tears. "Where could she be? Her bed is empty, and the gun is missing."

The flames were dying out and the smoke thickened around them. "We caught this in time," Russ said. "Now we have to find Bella."

Maggie ran into the house to get flashlights, and after checking inside the barn, both of them began searching around in the yard.

When Boney let out a weak, feeble moan, Russell made his way over into the weeds and tall grass. He saw Bella's face covered in blood. Boney lay a few feet away and was bleeding profusely.

"Oh, God, no," Russell said to himself. Aloud he shouted, "Maggie, she's over here." Her pulse was strong, but he couldn't rouse her. "Quick, help me get her into the truck."

The two of them gently lifted Bella and then Boney into the truck, and they sped toward town.

∼

Maggie stood at the side of Bella's hospital bed and held her great-grandmother's blue-veined hand. She had always thought those hands were the most beautiful she had ever seen. Even at her advanced age, she kept them soft, and the nails on her slender fingers were well manicured and tapered at the ends.

The long ride down the winding road to the nearest hospital in Taos was almost unbearable for Maggie. Her precious Bella remained unconscious and bleeding from a wound to her face and head. The doctor was optimistic but cautious. The CT scan had come back normal and showed no bleeding in her brain, but due to her age, there could always be complications.

Bella was sleeping and breathing oxygen through the soft cannulas in her nostrils.

She had inhaled smoke, but thankfully she had not been burned in the fire. Maggie knew if she and Russell had stayed for the dessert that they had both declined or had left the restaurant even five minutes later than they did, they would have been too late to save Bella and the barn.

∼

After the doctors at the hospital determined that Bella was no longer critical, Russell left to check on Boney at the veterinarian's office in Angel Falls. Maggie thought he acted as if he couldn't get out of the hospital fast enough, but she was worried about Boney, also. About an hour after he left, he called her.

"The news is not good," he said. "I'm sorry."

"Oh, no. Not Boney," Maggie said. "Is he dead?"

"No, but he's in surgery, and the doc says it's touch and go."

Maggie's voice broke, and a sob escaped.

"It will be a miracle if he makes it through this, Maggie. He may not be able to walk. That bastard shot him in the back leg. He's lost a lot of blood."

"Tell the vet to save that bullet. The feds said they're going to comb the ground out there looking for tire tracks and any other evidence they can find. Bella is a legend in these parts, and they're not going to let this one go. Somebody's going to pay."

"How's Bella?" he asked.

She noticed the tremor in his voice and hurried to reassure him. "She's strong, and her lungs are healthy. All those years of living a healthy life paid off big time. The doctors are hesitant to say she is out of the woods because of her age, but I know Bella, and she's a fighter."

"Did she break anything when they knocked her down? I still can't believe anyone would manhandle an old woman."

"There's nothing broken, thank God, but she has several contusions. The worst one is on her hip. Walking will be painful for a few weeks."

"Maggie, if you don't have any objection to my staying in the cabin for a while, I don't plan to leave until these bastards are behind bars." His voice rang with command.

Maggie sighed. "I'd like that."

CHAPTER 10

Russell sat on a hard, plastic chair in the empty waiting room of the emergency vet clinic. Boney had been in surgery for over an hour, and the last update was not promising. Russell had never owned a dog growing up and had been too consumed by his career to care for one as an adult. Boney had worked his way right into his heart, and he was praying the ugly mutt would pull through.

He was worried about Bella too. Again, he had no point of reference. He didn't come from a happy home and never had an extended family either. There had only been his father, stepmother, and stepbrother. Bella was a feisty old lady with a beautiful soul. Magdalena would be devastated if anything happened to her great-grandmother.

Whenever he closed his eyes, all he could see was the fire. No one had died this time, but Bella could have. If he hadn't taken Magdalena out for dinner, he would have been there to protect her. He was poison to the people he loved. He hung his head and looked down at the speckled tiled floor as unwanted memories of another fire filled his head. Memories he had tried to outrun for the last few months had caught up with him.

He looked up when a man in scrubs came out into the waiting room. He was a young guy who didn't look old enough to be out of high school much less to have a veterinarian degree.

"Mr. Murphy, barring any unexpected complications, your dog should recover. As I told you earlier, he lost a lot of blood, and I didn't know if we would have to amputate the back leg or not. We were able to save it for now. He will have a difficult recovery, but he will get better."

"Thank you, doctor. That is terrific news." A rush of relief engulfed him, and tears sprang into his eyes. *Damn dog*, he thought.

"He'll be here for quite some time. At least a week. You can talk to Lydia at the front desk, and she can work out a payment plan for you."

Russell settled the initial bill with a credit card and asked to use the phone. He hadn't brought a cell phone with him when he'd left Albuquerque. He'd only planned on being away a few days, but those days turned into weeks and then to months.

Maggie answered on the first ring. "How's Boney? Did he make it through surgery?"

"Yes, the doctor says he's going to pull through. I'll give you all the details when I see you. How is Bella?"

She woke up for a few minutes, but she was pretty incoherent. "She's sleeping now. Will you be back soon?" Russell could hear the longing in her voice. Magdalena wasn't the kind of woman that asked for support, but in her own way, she was asking for his.

"Yes, I'm leaving now."

~

MAGDALENA'S FACE showed the toll the night had taken on her. She had carelessly pulled back her black hair, and tendrils had escaped and were touching her cheeks.

Smudges had begun to form under her dark, somber eyes. She was still beautiful, Russell thought.

"Hi," he said and walked softly into the room. "You look really tired. I can sit with Bella if you want to try to take a nap."

"No, I want to be right here beside her when she wakes up. She will be confused, and I don't want her to be afraid." She wiped a tear from her eye and said, "She could have died, Russ. What kind of man could do this to an eighty-five-year-old woman?"

Russ shook his head and pulled a chair up next to her. "The only thing they were thinking about was getting the hell out of there after Bella confronted them with that shotgun. She was nothing more than collateral damage to them."

"And that makes it okay?"

"No, of course not. That's not what I meant. They assumed it would be a quick in and out and weren't expecting any resistance." He touched the old woman's face affectionately and said, "They weren't expecting Bella to fight back."

Russ closed his eyes and rubbed them. It was about four in the morning now, and he was bone tired. For a night that had started great, it sure had ended tragically, he thought. "What needs to be done?" he said.

"The horses must be fed, and when it gets light, I need to call the insurance adjustors."

Russell turned when the door opened. He expected to see a nurse and was pleased it was Wanda Eastman.

She opened her arms and Maggie immediately sank into them. "I'm so sorry, honey. I can't believe this has happened to Bella."

"How did you know?"

Wanda pointed to Russell and said, "He left a message on the store's emergency line. Hardly ever rings except when those squirrels got in the attic and set off the alarm a couple of years back. I came as soon as I could."

Wanda hugged Maggie and patted her on the back. "How is our Bella? What do the doctors say?"

"There hasn't been any brain damage, but she has a concussion, and of course her poor little body has been battered and bruised. She hasn't come out of it and has been mostly sleeping."

"She needs her rest to heal. As you know, she was one of the first ones to offer support when John had his heart attack. She and your granddaddy have always had a special place in my heart, and you know how I felt about your mama."

"Thank you for coming, Mrs. Eastman."

"Don't you worry about a thing. I sent Roddy out to your place to take care of the horses and make sure everything is locked up nice and tight, so you can concentrate on Bella."

Bella's paper-thin eyelids fluttered, and Russell quickly took her hand. "Magdalena, I think she's waking up."

"Hey there," Maggie said lovingly. "Welcome back."

"Mija, what happened?" the old woman said as her eyes moved from Maggie to Wanda and then to Russ.

"You were hurt, and you're in the hospital. What do you remember?"

"Boney was barking. Those men were going to burn down my barn."

"Yes, but you ran them off," Russell said and gave her hand a gentle squeeze.

"They shot Boney. Is … he?" Her voice was hoarse and weak as if she'd exerted all the strength she had to speak.

"He's going to be fine. He's at the vet's office, and they said he would make a full recovery." That wasn't exactly what the vet had said, but Bella didn't need to know what the extent of his injury was right now. It could wait until she was stronger, Russell thought.

~

WITH WANDA THERE, Russell felt he could get away for a few hours on the pretext that he was going to check on things, shower, and change clothes. Both his and Magdalena's clothes were covered in soot and smelled like smoke. She'd asked him to grab anything that matched out of her closet, but Russell had a stop he needed to make first.

He opened the door to City Hall and asked to speak to the mayor. A big-bosomed woman with platinum blonde hair greeted him suspiciously after taking in his appearance.

"Do you have an appointment?"

"No, but I'm sure Mayor O'Dell will want to see me. Is

that his office right there?" Russell pointed to a closed door behind the woman's desk. The sign on it read *Private*.

He started toward the door, and the flustered woman hurried after him. Russell opened the door and turned to the blonde and pointed to the sign. "This is a private conversation."

He pulled the door shut behind him and watched as O'Dell moved his swivel chair around and placed the phone on the receiver. When he stood, Russell planted a fist angrily against the side of O'Dell's jaw sending the man to the floor.

"What the hell?" he sputtered as blood seeped from his cut lip.

"Get up, you miserable coward, so that I can hit you again."

"I'll call the police and have you arrested. You've assaulted me." Then he yelled, "Simone, Simone."

"You think you can assault a harmless old woman and get away with it? You tried to destroy her home and nearly killed her." Russell stood over O'Dell, his fist clenched and his eyes blazing.

"I … I … don't know what you're talking about. What old woman? Are you talking about Bella?"

"Don't act so innocent. You've been trying to ruin her for a considerable amount of time according to Magdalena. This time you've gone too far. Get up damn it."

O'Dell put his arms out in front of him as if to push Russell away and scooted back against the wall. "I would never hurt Bella. I admire the old crone even if she doesn't like me very much. What happened?"

Either the man was a damn good actor, or he really didn't know what happened at the lodge. "Someone planned to burn the barn down last night, and Bella tried to stop them. She's in the hospital."

"Oh my God," O'Dell said rubbing his injured face. "I swear I knew nothing about it."

Simone began to pound on the door. "Lyman, Lyman are you okay? Do I need to call the police?"

Lyman glared at Russell but shook his head. "No, it's all right. Go on back to work. Everything's okay." Then he asked, "Was she seriously hurt?"

"She's an old woman. Of course, she's seriously hurt. You're a pretty pitiful excuse for a man."

When Russell turned to leave, Lyman called after him. "I won't forget this, Murphy."

Russell shrugged off the threat. He'd wanted to pound that man's face ever since he'd met him.

CHAPTER 11

Russell pulled up into the yard and parked beside a newer model pickup that presumably belonged to Roddy. He looked around and saw the tall, wiry man dusting hay off his jeans and walking toward him.

"It's a pretty big mess, huh?" Roddy said.

Russell nodded as he took in the portions of the barn that were charred. "Yeah, it looks bad. If Magdalena and I hadn't come home when we did … well, I don't want to even think about what would have happened to Bella. As for the property, with everything being so dry, the whole place could have gone up."

"I talked to my mom a little while ago. She said Bella is doing well considering her age and all. I bet Mags is going crazy blaming herself," Roddy said.

"Yes, she's beating herself up pretty good, and so am I. We should never have left Bella alone."

"You couldn't have known what would happen. I hope

the sheriff will do his job now and find the person responsible," Roddy said.

"He's no longer in charge of the case," Russell said. "ATF has taken over."

"I know Maggie thinks it's Lyman, and I guess it could be, but man that's just plain crazy. Anyone from around here knows you don't ever start any kind of fire. The whole forest could have gone up."

Roddy ran his fingers through his hair and sighed, "Hey, Murphy, I want to apologize for the other day. I was only messing with you, but my mom pointed out that you might have taken me seriously."

Suddenly uncomfortable, Russell said, "Okay, no problem." Then he looked in the direction of the open door. "What are you doing in the barn?"

"I was moving over the hay bales that are still good to the part of the barn that wasn't damaged."

"I came back to shower and change. I'll give you a hand before I do."

Although the morning was chilly, Russell was down to short sleeves after several minutes of piling bales in the corner and stopped to wipe the sweat from his eyes. He could smell the wet hay that would be worthless now. "It's fortunate that you're in Angel Falls today, so you can help Magdalena. She said you're a lawyer in Albuquerque. I imagine it was difficult to get away."

"Not so much. I didn't have any big trials going on, and there's never a shortage of clients for a criminal attorney. After Dad had his heart attack, he had to have surgery. Thankfully, the hospital was in Albuquerque. When the doctor released him to come home, I felt I needed to be here for a little while. The whole thing was pretty scary, you know, I could have lost my dad."

Russell did know how it felt to lose his dad, but when his father had died from cirrhosis caused by years of reckless drinking, all he felt was relief. He'd sent money to his stepmother for the funeral but didn't attend.

"I can stay another few days if need be to help out Maggie."

"I don't think she will leave Bella's side anytime soon," Russell said, "but I should be able to hold down everything here until they get back." He said the words tentatively as if testing the idea.

Roddy's expression stilled and became serious. "I would do anything for Maggie as I'm sure she would for me, but there isn't anything going on between us."

Russell didn't react, but he wanted to ask if the two old friends had once been lovers. There was an easy familiarity between them that Russell envied.

Roddy rested his foot on the hay and peeled off one of his gloves to pull back a lock of his hair that had plopped down onto his face. He chuckled and said, "I kissed Maggie when we were about thirteen or fourteen. Was like kissing my sister, and I have a sister, so I'd know."

Russell held Roddy's gaze across the stack of hay but did not respond.

"She wiped it right off and told me if I ever did that again she'd punch me." He paused and smiled. "I thought that was something I should tell you. I love Mags. She's family to me, so you better not hurt her."

"What are you talking about? There's nothing between Magdalena and me except friendship."

"Yeah, keep telling yourself that and see how it works out for you."

With that, Roddy turned back to his work in the barn as Russell, with a puzzled look, decided it was time to go and clean himself up.

~

Russell quickly showered and shaved. He'd been forced by necessity to buy additional clothing after he left Lyman's office. Everything he owned was either in the laundry or on his back.

As he buttoned the stiff new Levi's, Roddy's voice echoed through his brain. Did he have feelings for Magdalena? Of course, he did. She was kind, and caring, and smoking hot. He wanted to hold her and kiss her and tell her everything would be all right. But he wasn't the man for her. She deserved someone that could and would be honest with her. He had been in Angel Falls much longer than he intended, but the pull the woman had on him was magnetic. Maybe she was a witch too, like Bella.

He moved his meager belongings into one of the spare bedrooms upstairs. He didn't intend to leave the two women alone until the sheriff caught the arsonists. When he left, if need be, he would hire someone to guard them. He meant what he said when he told Magdalena that he could afford to pay for dinner. Hell, he could afford to pay for a thousand dinners. Money was not an issue, but as he knew all too well, it could not buy happiness.

He found her bedroom and moved inside to gather her clothes. The bed was neatly made and covered by a chocolate, beige, and turquoise colored quilt sitting below a simple pine headboard. Her closet was arranged with blouses and dresses on one side and pants and skirts on the other. He pulled down a dark blue corduroy blouse and a pair of denim jeans. He loved her in blue. The color made her dark eyes pop.

She hadn't said anything about underwear, and he felt like a voyeur going through her dresser. His rough hands found a pair of silky pink panties and a matching bra. He picked them up and changed his mind and put them back while trying hard to block the image of what it would be like to take them off of her. He ended up settling for plain white garments.

On the drive back to Taos, the image of fire kept sweeping through his mind. He felt anxious and wanted to get away from anything that reminded him of his past. He could drop the truck off at the hospital and tell Magdalena that he had to leave. Then, he could disappear into the mountains again where he could try to find peace.

He hit the steering wheel and moaned. Who was he trying to fool? He wasn't going anywhere. It was time to come clean with Magdalena as soon as the time was right after Bella was home and on the mend.

∽

LYMAN UNTANGLED himself from his blonde bombshell secretary and reached for his ringing phone. She'd been comforting him in all the right places after his encounter with the drifter that morning. His jaw ached, and he was pretty sure a couple of his teeth were loose.

Simone kept asking him why he hadn't called the

police. He didn't because the publicity would be terrible, and he could only imagine the headlines. *Mayor assaulted and accused of arson.* Even if people didn't believe it, the accusation would be out there. Bella Morales was very well respected.

He recognized the number and growled a terse, "Hello." He listened for a few seconds and said, "Hold on a minute."

"Simone, this is an important call. I need some privacy." She gave him a warm kiss on the mouth and left the room in a huff.

"Do you have any idea what you did?" Lyman said trying to keep his voice at a level that couldn't be heard in the outer office. "You assaulted an old woman and tried to catch the whole countryside on fire. Are you stupid or just plain crazy?"

"Things aren't working out so well between you and the organization, Mr. O'Dell. You aren't living up to your end of the bargain. My employer realizes that sometimes collateral damage is necessary. Mrs. Morales has lived a long and happy life. Sometimes lives are lost or sacrificed."

"I have done everything you asked of me. I can't help it if the old lady is stubborn."

"Mr. O'Dell, I don't think you completely understand the situation you're in. I am not only talking about her life." The voice was silent and then said, "You do value your life don't you, Mr. O'Dell?"

Lyman broke out in a sweat and began to pace back and forth. "Look, I'll find some other way to pay back the money I owe."

"Five hundred thousand dollars in cash? If you say so,

Mr. O'Dell. You have one week to come up with either the money or the land. I would hate for one of your constituents to find your mutilated body. You understand we'd have to make an example of you."

Lyman held the phone in a death grip and sucked in a panicked breath. "Please I …," but the line went dead.

CHAPTER 12

Dr. Reid walked into the room with a huge smile on his chubby, round face. "Good morning, Mrs. Morales. I think we can spring you today. I've received glowing reports from the physical therapist and from your granddaughter. Magdalena assures me that you will not be left alone once you go home."

Maggie had washed Bella's beautiful silver hair and pulled it up in a loose knot on top of her head. The bruises on her face had faded to a dark purple, as the cuts and abrasions began to heal. Bella sat up and smiled. "Thank you, doctor. You and your staff have given me excellent care, and I appreciate your kindness. I will be glad to be going home."

"I want you to take it easy. No riding around on horses or in vehicles. Not until you are completely healed. It is a testament to your excellent physical health that no bones were broken."

"And to my hard head, I think. My Reggie always said

it was good he married me because I'd be a thorn in any other man's side."

Maggie chuckled and said, "I'm afraid that's a trait that all the Morales women have. I will take excellent care of her. I promise."

When they were alone, Maggie sat on the bed and gently folded Bella's hands in hers. "You're not afraid to go home, are you? I've asked Russell to move into the main house."

"No, mija, I am ready to meet my maker anytime He comes calling. I do not fear death, but I think I will stick around a little while longer. I have a few things left to do. I'm glad that Russell will be there to help protect you although you are a fierce girl, my Maggie. I feel sorry for anyone that goes up against you. My son taught you very well."

Both women looked toward the door when they heard a soft knock. Agent Matt Bentley from the Alcohol Tobacco and Firearms Bureau stuck his head in the door. "Good morning," he said. "If you're up to it, I'd like to ask you a couple more questions about the men that assaulted you." The agent had been at the hospital the morning after the fire and asked Maggie, Bella, and Russell endless questions.

"Sit down, Agent Bentley," Bella said. "I don't know what more I can tell you."

"I have a couple of pictures for you to look at and tell me if you recognize the people in them." He laid both pictures on the tray next to her bed and moved it toward her, so she could see better.

Bella put on her glasses and stared at the subjects in each photo while taking in their features and facial structure. She pointed to a dark-haired white man with a scruffy beard and pocked face. "This looks like the man that pushed me. With the light from the blazing fire, I got a pretty good look. I didn't see the other one's face well, but he was tall and thin. Latino, I think."

Maggie quickly moved behind the agent while looking over his shoulder. "Did you catch them? What did they say?"

"Unfortunately, they didn't say anything. Their bodies were found inside a truck at a rest stop on I-25. The state police identified them by fingerprints. The information came across my desk because of their priors for arson. On a hunch, I thought I'd see if Mrs. Morales recognized them."

"Who were they?" Maggie said as she took Bella's hand.

"A couple of ex-cons from Springer. It looked pretty much like a professional hit."

"Now, maybe the sheriff will believe me," Maggie said with exasperation. "Someone is trying to force Bella and me off our land. If this weren't the twenty-first century, I would swear we were in the Wild West with some land baron trying to run off the little guy."

"And who do you think is behind this?"

"All I know is for the past few months, even before the vandalism, Lyman O'Dell, my ex-husband, has been trying to buy the land."

"What about that young fella you got staying out there that I interviewed. He arrived shortly after the vandalism started if I recall correctly."

Bella spoke so softly that Bentley had to lean closer to

hear. "Russell did not try to harm me. His heart is pure. No, Agent Bentley. You need to look elsewhere."

His expression said he thought otherwise, but he did not challenge her statement. "I also checked into the information you gave me about your manager, Marty Chavez. The autopsy results indicated the cause of death was blunt force trauma to the head. I know the sheriff thought it was an accident, but the man didn't drown or have a heart attack. There was no water in his lungs. It looks like he was murdered."

~

Bella was dressed and sitting in a chair when Russell arrived to drive Magdalena and her home. He looked around the tiny room and then at Bella. "Where's Magdalena?"

"I love that you call her by her full name. Her mother did the same. To me, she was the little girl in pigtails running around my garden. My Maggie." She held out her hand to Russell and motioned for him to come to her.

"I asked Maggie to take care of all the checkout and insurance stuff. She'll be back in a little while. That will give me time to talk to you."

Russell pulled up a chair and sat beside her and she took his hands. Her hands felt soft and warm.

"You've had a tragic life, haven't you? But you are a good man," Bella said.

He cleared his throat and started to get up. "I need to go see where the nurse is with the proverbial wheelchair, so we can get you out of here."

"Russell, sometimes the spirit needs to be set free.

Keep it close in your heart but don't be smothered by it." Russell sat back down and swallowed a sudden lump in his throat.

"Everything that happens is God's plan," Bella continued. "We may not like or agree with it, but that is the way it must be. You can't run away forever. Unburden your soul, and it will set you free."

Fleeing the room as quickly as possible, he almost ran Magdalena down. "I'm sorry, I ... I need to find the nurse," he said as he hurried past her.

Maggie took one look at her great-grandmother's face and she knew. "Bella, what did you do?"

She smiled softly and said, "What needed to be done."

～

AFTER BELLA WAS fast asleep in her own bed, Maggie fixed two large cups of hot chocolate and handed one to Russ. The fire he had started earlier burned brightly as orange and blue flames leapt from the large aspen logs he'd chopped fiercely after they arrived home.

"What's wrong, Russ?" She put her hand up to silence him. "And don't tell me you're worried about Bella or the lodge. I think I know you well enough by now to know it's something else. What's really going on with you?"

Staring into the fire, he moved closer to the hearth with his back to Maggie. It was time, he thought. She deserved the truth. He turned to face her and found compassion in her dark eyes. "I was married, and I had a daughter. They both died about six months ago in a fire. I guess what happened to Bella has brought everything back, not that it ever goes away."

Maggie was silent and continued to watch the brawny man in front of her. "Do you want to talk about it?"

"No, but Bella told me I need to, and that if I do, it will set me free. The thing is, what if I don't want to be set free?" Maggie's soft eyes encouraged him to continue.

"My wife was having an affair. I didn't blame her. I worked too much. Too many hours. She wanted a divorce. Strangely, instead of feeling desolate, I was glad. We'd never been good together. The only good thing was our daughter." He turned, and Maggie could see the tears in his eyes.

"I loved her so much. She was only five when she died, and it was my fault. My wife was leaving and taking her, and that was something I couldn't abide. I was willing to fight for custody. I was willing to give up everything I owned to keep Emma."

The cup slipped from Maggie's hand and fractured into pieces on the polished hardwood floor. Her heart thumped, and her mouth went dry. She reached down to pick up the scattered shards and cried out as she pulled her fingers away wet with blood.

Russell turned sharply and stooped down to gather Maggie in his arms. "I'm sorry. I didn't mean to upset you. I shouldn't have said anything. I ... I ... think I should leave."

Maggie forcefully clung to him her hands digging into his shoulders leaving red splotches on his shirt. "No, no, you can't leave. I've got to tell you something, and I don't think you're going to believe me."

They sat together on the sofa, and Russell said, "Tell me."

"About six months ago, I started to have a dream. Not

a single night has passed, without my having the same vision. I'm in the forest, and it's green and lush. The sun is shining, and I'm truly happy. A little girl with dark, curly hair and blue eyes is giggling and running through the pines, and I pick her up and say, "I love you, Emma." And she says, "I love you, Mama. When can I see you? Can you hurry please?"

Russell pulled away and said, "What is this some kind of sick joke?"

"No," she said alarmed. "Why would I do that? You can ask Bella. It's the truth."

Russell got up and paced back in forth by the fire running his fingers through his hair. "This doesn't make any sense. It has to be some kind of coincidence. Emma's hair wasn't dark. You weren't dreaming about my daughter."

"I didn't say I was. All I can tell you is my dreams started about six months ago about the same time your Emma died. Do I know what that means? Hell no," she said throwing her hands up in exasperation. "I've got to put something on my finger. I'm still bleeding."

Maggie got up and went to the kitchen to wash her hand under the faucet. Several moments later Russell joined her, his arms snaking around her and his head resting on her shoulder. "I'm sorry."

She hesitated and then reached back and squeezed his hand.

~

THEY SAT WRAPPED in a blanket on the floor with the fire only embers now. Russell touched her hair and ran the silky strands through his fingers. They'd hardly spoken, but both felt an urgent need to touch and stay connected. "I couldn't stay after the funeral. I left my business in the capable hands of my partner and left. I only intended to be away for a few days, but I found I couldn't go back."

"Emma was supposed to be with me that night, and if she had been, she would still be alive. Everything is a blur, and I don't remember much except getting very drunk. I didn't want my wife, Sarah, to take Emma away from me."

Russell turned toward her, and huskiness lingered in his voice. "I don't deserve to be happy. Why should I be allowed to be happy when my little girl is gone?"

Maggie ran her hands over his face and kissed him very softly. "I know you think you don't deserve happiness, but you're wrong. You can't punish yourself for the rest of your life for one mistake."

"I don't want to love anyone or anything ever again."

"I know you don't," she said kissing him again.

"I don't want to love you, Magdalena, or Bella, or your dumb dog."

"I know."

"I don't know what connection you have with my daughter. I don't understand any of this, but God, I need you so much, Magdalena." He trembled and held her tightly.

Again, she only said, "I know."

He kissed her then the way he'd wanted to since he saw her standing in her yard with a pistol on her waist and a shotgun in her hands. She had looked magnificent with her windblown, flyaway hair reflected in the late afternoon sun and her dark, passionate eyes staring at him.

He felt her lips pressing into his and heard her moan softly. He wanted her to stop him, but when she didn't, he kissed her harder and forcefully pushed her down onto the rug in front of the fire.

"Tell me no," he said. "Please, tell me no."

"Oh, Russell, forgive yourself and love me. Let's heal each other."

She put her hands underneath his shirt, and he shivered not from the cold but from passion. He let her be the aggressor now and take them wherever she wanted. Their lovemaking was fierce and frenzied as if the act would drive away all the ghosts of the past and leave only the present. With this woman, he believed all things were possible.

CHAPTER 13

Maggie was humming in the kitchen when Bella ambled into the room. "What are you doing out of bed. I didn't even know you were awake." She rushed to her great-grandmother and helped her into a kitchen chair.

"Don't fuss," said Bella. "I want breakfast and a cup of coffee. I can spend my time sleeping when I'm dead. You're in a good mood this morning. Did you have a nice night?"

Maggie blushed and turned toward the coffee maker. "You know I did. I've never been able to keep anything from you."

"Even a blind person could see it was only a matter of time. Where is he anyway?"

"He went upstairs to take a shower after he took care of the horses. He'll be down in a minute."

"Hmm," Bella said, taking a sip of the coffee Maggie put in front of her. "I think I will have a big breakfast."

"You never eat a big breakfast."

"Never is a long time, mija. Today I want a big breakfast. Eggs, bacon, toast, and some of my homemade jelly." Bella patted her stomach. "I have lost a few pounds."

"Then I've found them," Russell said as he silently entered the room.

"For such a big man, you are very stealthy, Mr. Murphy," Bella chuckled. "Perhaps you should make my breakfast."

"Perhaps I should."

"You can cook?" Maggie said with a warm smile.

"A little."

"What's a little?"

"When I was fifteen, I went to work as a busboy at Pete's Diner and moved right on up to fry cook when I was sixteen. I can make a mean green chile hamburger, and I'm not too bad with over-easy eggs."

"Tell me," Bella said. "I want to know about this boy named Russell who's captured my Maggie's heart."

"Hey, don't look at me," Maggie said. "I didn't say a word to her." She leaned down and whispered to Russell loud enough for Bella to hear. "Remember she rides a broomstick and wears a pointed hat."

"I was a very boring teenager, Bella," said Russell. "I went to school, to the library, and to work. I tried to stay away from home as much as possible." He got bacon and a carton of eggs out of the refrigerator and slid the bacon expertly onto the electric grill. My dad was a drunk and not one of those men that was the happy, joyous, life of the party kind. He was mean and loved to abuse anyone weaker or smaller. Unfortunately, my stepmother took the brunt of his rage. Who knows? Maybe that's why my own mother took off when I was young. I only wish she'd bothered to take me with her."

Maggie placed slices of bread in the toaster and turned away before Russ could see the sympathy in her eyes. She knew he wouldn't like that.

"Do you remember your mother?" Bella asked.

"Yeah, a little. She was nice and smelled good. I remember she used to hide my books when Dad came home drunk. He didn't want me to read and would throw them away if he saw them." He moved the bacon over, cracked four eggs, and turned to Bella. "I haven't thought of that in years. I guess I'm so angry at her that I only think of the negative and not the positive."

Bella set her cup down and said, "Russell?" When she had his attention, she pursed her lips, tapped them with her finger and said, "Did you ever think that maybe she didn't leave you?"

"Of course, she did. Dad said she … my God, I never thought. Do you think he hurt her or that …?"

He had a hard time getting the words out, so Bella finished for him. "Killed her?"

Russell handed the spatula to Maggie and sat down beside Bella. "Do you know something?"

"Do I know something that you can prove? No. Do I feel something? Yes, from the first time I held your hand. I'm sure last night you told Maggie the rest of your secrets."

"Do you know about Emma?"

"Yes, Maggie tells me about her dreams."

"No, I mean my Emma. My daughter that died."

"So, there it is, the connection," Bella said. "I knew it was there when I asked you to stay."

Maggie placed a plate of eggs and bacon in front of Bella and said, "I'm guessing you knew when you woke up this morning that this was going to happen."

Bella only smiled and said, "I'm getting tired. After I eat, I think I will rest awhile."

∼

"So, you've dealt with this your whole life. Does she always know everyone's secrets?" Russell said as they walked briskly toward the barn. Maggie had looked at the damage briefly when they arrived yesterday, and the sight had made her sick.

"No, if she did, my mother wouldn't have run off to California and married my loser father, and I wouldn't have married my loser, Lyman. She can't predict the future, but she has strong feelings about things. I can't explain it. She's been that way forever. Did she know that my mom would die or that her son would also? If she did know, she never told anyone."

Maggie looked up at the charred structure and wiped away tears. "I don't know how we will ever get this repaired before winter."

"What did the insurance adjuster say?"

"There's a little problem. Along with not paying the taxes, Papa Ernesto also let the insurance lapse."

Russell pulled her to him and said, "Magdalena, no." He cupped her face and looked into her eyes. "Don't worry. I've got money."

"I won't take your money, and neither will Bella. That is a very generous offer but …"

"You're not listening, I've got lots of money. More than I know what to do with."

Maggie stepped back and looked up into the crystal blue of his eyes. "You're not kidding, are you? What'd you do rob a bank?"

"No," he laughed, "of course not. When I graduated, I started a company with my roommate. We develop software solutions and software systems for industries."

"And there's money in that?"

"As it turns out, yes there is. That's what destroyed my marriage. I was spending all of my time trying to make more money. I never had anything growing up, and I wanted Emma to have the world." He sighed and dropped his hands, "Money doesn't mean very much to me anymore."

"It doesn't matter, Russ, I still can't take your money."

"Then I'll loan it to you with interest. We can draw up a contract. This is Bella's home. Your home. Let me do this one thing for you."

"I don't know, I'll have to talk to Bella. She's a woman with fierce pride."

"Yes, she is, but not a stupid one."

Maggie looked toward the pen with the horses. "We use the horses in the winter for sleigh rides and in the summer for trail rides. Do you ride?"

"Nope, not even a little."

"Do you want to learn?"

"Hell no," he said shaking his head.

"But you will, won't you?"

She showed Russell how to bridle and saddle the horse. April was a sweet old mare that had been around since Maggie was a teenager. After a couple of trots around the yard, Maggie assured Russell he rode like a pro.

They took a short ride down a little path in front of the lake and stopped. Russell climbed down from the horse and stretched. "How did people do this before cars were invented?"

"You'll get used to it. You're using muscles you haven't used before."

"Yeah, like my butt muscle."

"Come on, you baby," Maggie said taking his hand.

"It's really pretty down here. How much land do you have?"

"About thirty acres. This isn't a lake. It's more like a pond, but we're able to put paddle boats in the water during the summer, and our guests can catch fish."

"No wonder someone wants this property. How did your family end up with it anyway?"

"Land grants back in the eighteen hundreds. Since then, most of the original land was divided between heirs, sold, or taken over by the Forest Service."

"What a proud heritage you have, Magdalena. This is more than just land to you."

"Oh, yes, it is. Strange that you understand that."

"I really have no family," Russell said. "I envy the roots you have. My father's family is gone, I suppose. I never knew my grandparents, and if I had aunts and uncles, they were never mentioned. Of course, I know absolutely nothing about my mother."

"You said you have a stepmother?"

"Yes, and a stepbrother, Hugh. I was eleven when they moved in, and Hugh was around three. I think my dad mostly left him alone. I really don't know what happened after I went to college. I never went back home."

"Nancy, my stepmother, called me a few years back and said Hugh had gotten into trouble and was running around with the wrong crowd. I gave him a job with my company, and he seems to be doing okay."

"Are you close?"

"I guess. He's the closest thing to family I have, so I've included him in my life, you know on holidays and special occasions."

Maggie threw a rock and watched it skip across the water. She never tired of looking at the blue sky and the shimmering blue water below surrounded by shrubs, trees, and the tall grass turned brown by the cold nights.

"So, what's he doing now?"

"I have no idea. How selfish of me. Hugh adored Emma and got along well with Sarah. I didn't even think about him when I left. I was too self-absorbed."

"Don't be too hard on yourself." Maggie turned toward him and touched his arm. "You were trying to deal with a terrible tragedy in the best way you could. I can understand completely. When Papa Ernesto died so suddenly, I felt like I'd lost my rudder. With my mother's death, I had time to grasp what was coming."

Maggie turned and clasped both of his arms while looking directly into his eyes. "I am in no way comparing what happened to me to the death of your daughter. I can't even imagine a loss like that."

Russell didn't reply, but the look in his eyes was gentle and understanding.

"I guess we'd better get back," Maggie said. "The ladies from the church we left with Bella will need to get home.

It's amazing what older women like to talk about. They'll discuss what doctor they saw last week, and what new ache or pain they've discovered. They must be utterly fascinated with Bella's story."

Russell laughed and took Maggie's hand as they walked back toward the horses. Before they mounted their horses, Russell pulled her close and kissed her softly. "Last night was amazing. You're amazing. Thank you for being so patient and not pressuring me to tell you about my life. I wasn't ready to move forward before."

"And now you are?"

"I hope so. I really hope so," he said and pulled her close again for another kiss.

CHAPTER 14

The house was alive with the popping and creaking so common in older homes, and Maggie heard the furnace kick on as hot air rushed through the ducts. She lay curled up beside Russell in her bedroom where they'd been sleeping since Bella returned from the hospital. Russell slowly inched toward the side of the bed and had one foot on the floor when Maggie grasped his arm.

"Hey," she said in a sleepy drawl. "Where are you going?"

"I'm going upstairs; it's almost morning."

"You know you don't have to do that. I'm not seventeen and sneaking my boyfriend in through the window."

"Did you actually do that?"

"No, of course not. Papa Ernesto would have killed me, and such a thing honestly never occurred to me."

"It doesn't feel right sleeping with you when we are right next to Bella's room. Seems kind of disrespectful."

"Bella knows what's going on. Believe me; she'd say

something if she didn't approve. She chose you for me, Russ. She's given us her stamp of approval."

She sat up, and the sheet fell exposing her bare breast with her tousled dark hair spilling across one nipple. Russ reached over cupping and caressing it. "Maybe I don't have to leave yet."

She reached out to pull him closer and whispered, "No, not just yet."

∼

As the first rays of the sun filtered through the window, Maggie watched Russ leave her bed. Their relationship was so new that she had no idea where it was going. He was a complicated man, and although he had given her a glimpse into the real Russell Murphy, Maggie doubted he'd told her everything. That was one of the wonders of the connection she had with him.

Since the first night they'd made love, she hadn't dreamed of Emma. The little girl was gone from her dreams but not from her heart. She felt different but didn't know why. Maybe it was because she was happy for the first time in a long time with these feelings of contentment and peace. She would talk to Bella as soon as she could to search for the answer. She also needed to discuss the offer Russ had made for a loan. It went against everything she'd ever been taught. Pride ran deep in her family, and it wasn't easy to trust or depend on someone else.

Bella sat at her dressing table putting on touches of makeup. Her face was surprisingly unlined for a woman her age, and Maggie hoped she had inherited those good genes from her mother's side. She knew nothing of her father's family. He had never tried to contact her or her mother, Connie, since their return from California. Whenever she asked, her mother would say, "He didn't want us, and we are better off here." But Connie didn't love the land as much as Maggie did, and Maggie thought her mother only stayed to raise her. Connie Morales wasn't a happy woman, but Maggie knew she loved her daughter fiercely.

"Morning, Bella," Maggie said as she tapped softly on Bella's open door. "You look beautiful as always. Those ugly bruises are almost gone."

"Good morning, my heart," she said pulling her hair back from her face. "Yes, it's good. I hate it when people refer to me as fragile and tiptoe around my feelings. I'm old, but I'm not dead yet. I have a few things left to do with my life."

She turned and gave Maggie a radiant smile. "You look very content ... no not content," she pressed her lips together and steepled her fingers under them, "a better word would be satisfied."

She turned back to the mirror and applied a light brush of foundation and blush and a hint of pink on her lips. "I sent Russell to town to pick up our Boney. He needs to be home now instead of in a cold, sterile cage."

"Is he ready to be released? Did the vet call?"

"Yes, he is, and no we haven't received a call."

"But you know he's ready. Of course, you do." Maggie put her hands out to help her great-grandmother to her feet.

Bella winced and softly said, "Getting old isn't fun, but it's better than not, don't you think? My hip still aches a little from the fall. I'd like to go for a nice, short walk. Me and Boney. He's going to have a pronounced limp from now on, but the doctor says he shouldn't be in any pain. We will make a matched pair."

Maggie didn't know what to say, so she changed the subject. "I'll get you a cup of coffee and something to eat."

"Already had coffee and already ate. Russell made me toast before he left. The poor man looked tired. You know anything about that?"

"You know I do," Maggie said as she left the room, her words trailing behind her.

Bella sat at the large table in the kitchen and shuffled and spread her cards across the surface. "You finally want a reading?"

"Yes," Maggie said meekly.

The first card she turned over was an old man with a long white beard. "Ah, you will be searching for the truth and find enlightenment. It says you are a wise woman. You will find answers to grasp success."

Maggie squirmed in her seat but knew better than to ask questions. The card's message would unfold, and questions could be asked at the end. The next card she turned over was the large roulette wheel.

"An excellent sign for you. There will be change and fortune in your destiny. Enjoy your new relationship and don't overthink. Life is a gamble and change is inevitable, but there will be stones in the road. Let's see what else you have."

"Of course, The Lovers," Bella sighed and put her hand over her heart. "You will find love, but more importantly you will find trust and respect. A perfect balance. I see you working together to overcome an obstacle."

The next card was the card of death, but Maggie had

known since she was a little girl that the Tarot never meant physical death. She looked up at Bella for an explanation.

"You will experience a huge change; I think for the better. Your life will never be the same. Your new path will give you unexpected joy."

When Maggie chose the last card, and Bella turned it over, the old woman's face lit up with pleasure. "See here," she pointed, "this shows creation and birth. It could mean a new life."

Maggie moved her hand to touch her stomach lightly. "Emma," she said in wonder.

∽

MAGGIE HAD a lot to think about when she walked out onto the front porch. After Bella's reading, she'd emptied her coffee down the drain and made a cup of herbal tea. November days were usually in the mid-forties, so she dressed in a long-sleeved flannel shirt and down vest. She got on the ATV and stopped at each cabin making a list of what needed to be done to get ready for the guests. She was more optimistic than she'd been over the last two seasons. Something was going to happen to make everything better, even though she didn't yet know what it was. There had been a slight dusting of snow earlier in the week and a few rain showers that had been absorbed quickly by the thirsty soil.

Her first stop was the small log cabin set apart from the others. This was where Dora and Billy Hansen lived during the four months of the winter season and the three months of the summer season. The older retired couple spent the remainder of their time living in Arizona with their daughter and grandchildren. Dora cooked for the guests and cleaned the cabins with the help of two girls from town. Billy kept all the winter gear used by guests in pristine condition and during the summer took care of the trail and hayrides as well as keeping the small paddle boats and fishing paraphernalia clean and in good repair.

They were deeply troubled when Maggie called to let them know about Marty's death. She hadn't wanted to call them again with the horrible news that he was murdered. His senseless death was still something Maggie couldn't understand, and she hoped to have more news when the couple arrived later this week. She didn't want to believe his death was connected to the vandalism occurring on the property. Why would Lyman want to hurt Marty? They'd never liked each other, but still.

She'd finished by looking at the last cabin. It was the one she and Russ had worked on side-by-side, and she felt great accomplishment. She smelled fresh paint as her boots clicked across the newly repaired tile. Most people would think she was crazy if she admitted that she liked the smell of paint. It brought back treasured memories of the time she spent with Papa Ernesto. He had always made sure she had her own paintbrush and her own special wall to paint. When she got older, she'd realized the poor man most likely had to paint over anything she'd done, but at that time, in those moments, she felt very special.

Tears formed in her eyes as she glanced around the room. "I miss you so much, Papa. You were too young to die. I'm trying to hold it all together for you, I really am, but it's so hard."

She heard the unmistakable sound of gravel crunching and realized Russ was back, and if Bella was correct, Boney was back too. She could see the old red truck parked in front of the house and steered the ATV in that direction. The truck had definitely seen better days, but one of the first things Maggie had done when money became tight was to sell her car. Since then, Papa Ernesto's truck that he used to call Old Red, got her where she needed to go which was never very far.

She saw Russ lean in and pick up the skinny dog and gently place him on the dry mountain grass. Boney's hind leg was encased in a black sleeve that started at his hip and ended above his left paw. When they'd visited the dog at the vets' office, he seemed so sad and lost, but now his tail was wagging, and as she got closer and turned off the engine, she could hear him whine.

She squatted in front of Boney and hugged him as his wet tongue slid all over her face. "I missed you too. You big old goofy boy."

She looked up at Russ and said, "What did the vet say? I was surprised when Bella said he was coming home today."

"Well, you know Bella. The vet said not to let him jump around and try to keep him quiet. If he's up to it, he can get limited exercise but no running. We have to keep the stitches dry and protected, thus the sleeve. I guess it beats wearing one of those cone things."

"Yeah, Boney would have hated that."

"What have you been up to since I left?" Russell said.

"Oh, not much. Took a shower, had some breakfast, had a reading."

"You what?"

"I needed to find out a few things, so I asked Bella."

"And, what'd she say?" He looked amused and maybe a little wary.

"That I'm going to meet a handsome stranger who walks off the mountain, and he'll sweep me off my feet. Oh, wait, that already happened."

"Smart alec. What did she really say?"

"You don't believe, so why should I tell you? She reached up and gave him a soft kiss and a punch on the arm."

"It's not that I don't believe, it's … well … I'm skeptical," Russ said.

"She said you were stubborn, had secrets and guilt … and you are, and you do. I have no idea what she told you in the hospital room, but it had you running out of there like your life depended on it."

"She told me about Emma, okay? Not in those words, but she knew. Damn, Magdalena, I don't want to believe in voodoo."

"It's all right. You don't have to. I'll believe for both of us. The good news is the future looks pretty bright. Changes are going to happen, and I am confident that we are going to have a good season. I also believe Bella may be receptive to your offer of a loan."

Maggie reached for his hand and said, "Let's take Boney in and go talk to her."

Boney seemed to be as delighted to see Bella as she was to see him. He thumped his tail, licked her arms and face and after three turns to find the right spot, settled in front of her chair close to the fire.

Maggie waited on the couch looking expectantly at Bella, and Russ sat in the easy chair next to her.

"So, what is it you need to tell me?" Bella said.

"Well, Russell has a proposition or rather a solution for us. We need to get … that is I need to get your approval."

"Uh huh, and what is this solution? Solution to what?" Bella said.

Maggie looked at Russell and nodded her encouragement.

"I'd like to loan you the money to make the repairs and get the lodge out of the red. And before you say no, let me explain," Russell said.

"Maggie, what is this? What have you not been telling me? You said Ernesto did not pay the taxes. Surely we have money for the taxes without begging to strangers."

Russell flinched as if he'd been kicked. Maggie saw the hurt expression on his face. He seemed to pull into himself and sat silently looking at Maggie.

"I'm sorry, Russell," Bella said. "That was not called for. Pride sometimes is not a good thing. My Reggie scolded me many times on how it would be my downfall. If we fought, it was always over that."

Russell sat quietly, not looking at her.

She reached over and touched him gently on the arm. "I apologize and believe me for an old woman set in my ways that is not easy. I can't, at least for now, take your money. And where would you get money to pay my taxes anyway?"

"I have money that I don't need, and you do. It's as simple as that. It would be like going to a bank and getting a loan."

"Not like going to Lyman's bank, I hope." She laughed

and then soberly said, "No, I won't take your money. I will find another way, and that's final."

She stood and shook her finger at Maggie. "Shame on you, girl. You should know better. I'm going now to take a nap." The old woman walked slowly out of the room with Boney limping close behind her toward the bedroom.

CHAPTER 15

Russell was up to his elbows in repairing shingles and resealing gaps on the roof of cabin number eight. A year ago, Russell couldn't have imagined he would be a general all-around handyman. He learned more in these last few weeks than he had in his entire life. Sure, he was a book-smart, highly educated, computer geek, but now he felt more well-rounded. The realization made him prouder than his fancy degree from MIT. He could ride a horse and shoot a gun. He was like, way cool.

He grinned down from his ladder and called out to Magdalena, "Hey, thank you."

"You're welcome, I think. What for?"

"For making me so cool."

"What the heck are you talking about, Russ? Is the air too thin up there or something? Are you Rocky Mountain high?"

"No, or at least I don't think so. Is that a real thing?"

Magdalena gave him a look like he was crazy and

threw an empty water bottle at him. "So, what makes you think you're cool?" she called up to him.

"Thanks to everything you've taught me, I could strap on my tool belt and work on any construction site while riding my horse and carrying."

"You're so full of shit, Murphy."

He wiggled his eyebrows at her and went back to work but looked up when he heard the rumble of an engine and saw an ancient Toyota truck pulling a trailer with a Harley Davidson atop it shining in the afternoon sun. "Man, that's sweet," he said. "Your first guest?"

"Nah, that's Dora and Billy up from Arizona. She's our cook and housekeeper, and he works with the equipment and anything else that needs to be done."

So, he's my replacement, Russell thought but didn't say it out loud. This was a good thing. He realized he couldn't stay here at Cielo Verde forever. He had a business to run, friends that would be worried about him, and a partner who would be ready to throttle him. He needed to tell Maggie, but it could wait a little bit longer.

~

"You're early," Maggie said walking up to the couple in front of their cabin. "I wasn't expecting you until the end of the week."

Dora reminded her of everyone's grandma. Short salt and pepper hair, warm brown eyes, and a muffin top figure. Billy was short, rail skinny, and his white hair was cut close to the scalp. He had a Santa Claus beard and mustache. They were a dear couple, and she hoped this wouldn't be their last season.

Billy eased out of the truck and stretched. "You'd think after all these years that ole road would get shorter, but it don't. How are you doing, Miss Maggie?"

Maggie hugged them both and pointed to Russell who had climbed down from the ladder and was walking toward them. "This is Russell Murphy. Russell, meet Dora and Billy Hansen. Russell is helping us out for a while since most of my regulars are gone and of course, Marty."

"Oh, honey," Dora said, "Billy and I are so sorry about Marty. He was such a sweet man."

"Was not," Billy said. "He was an old coot, but you couldn't find a more honest and loyal person."

"Was it a heart attack?" Dora said wiping a tear from her eye.

Maggie glanced at Russ and then back to Dora and took a deep breath. This was going to be hard. "No, it wasn't an accident. Someone killed him."

"No, that can't be true. Why would anyone want to do that?"

"Someone smashed his head in and left him in the water tank. I can only assume it had to be one of the men who has been trying to run us off. Maybe he saw something or heard something. I don't know, but I know it was my fault."

"Oh, honey, it wasn't your fault. He worked for you, and he loved you and Bella very much. He would have naturally wanted to protect you, but you had nothing to do with what some evil person did. What has the sheriff said?"

"Well, since the barn was burned, ATF has gotten involved and so old Barney Fife is keeping a low profile. I can't imagine why the people of this county elected him except that he rode in on Lyman's coattails. I don't think he can make a move unless Lyman approves it."

"Yep, your ex-husband is a charismatic, handsome, con man. Good thing your mama was already gone when he came into your life. I think she would have shot him."

"Well, I've had enough jawing," Billy said as he started to unload their things from the back.

"Here let me give you a hand," Russell said, "That's a fine-looking bike you have. Softail Heritage Special?"

"Yeah, 1997. You ride?"

"A little, but it's been a while."

"What'd Maggie say your name was? You look kind of familiar."

"You're not the first person who's said that. I guess I've got one of those faces. It's Russell Murphy."

"Hmm, doesn't sound familiar. Oh well, it will come to me."

While the men were unloading the truck and the motorcycle, Maggie hugged Dora again and said, "I am so glad to see you. Come up to the house as soon as you're settled and see Bella. She's had a rough go of it and seeing you will lift her spirits."

"Sure will. Why don't I fix supper for everyone? We stopped off at the store in town and got a few things. I know how much Bella likes my chicken and dumplings."

"That sounds wonderful. I'm pretty fond of them too. Bella said she was making a pie today. She likes to spoil Russ."

"Yes, I was going to ask about him. He seems like the strong silent type. Anything going on there?"

"Well, maybe, we'll see how things work out, and he talks a lot more when you get to know him. When we first met, I don't think he uttered a complete sentence of more than five words."

"Where'd he come from?"

"Up there," Maggie pointed toward the mountain. "I'm not kidding. He literally walked right off the mountain. I will tell you all about it later."

∽

AFTER SHE TOOK A QUICK SHOWER, Maggie entered the kitchen which smelled of thyme and basil, and freshly baked pie. Her hair, still damp, was pulled back in a long braid down her back. She saw Russ immediately. He sat quietly drinking a mug of beer next to Bella. Billy's doing, she thought. She'd never seen Russ with a beer before.

"Everything smells delicious. I worked right through lunch, so I'm starved," Maggie said.

"Sit down, hon, and I'll dish it up," Dora said.

"Not too much, I want to have room for Bella's pie."

"Russell?"

"Spread it thick. Maggie wouldn't let me have lunch either, and no matter how much I eat, I will still have room for pecan pie." He patted his flat stomach and grinned.

"So, Billy, why'd you guys get here two days early? Your text said you'd be arriving on Friday," Maggie said.

"Don't you watch the news in this house? Is your Dish broken?"

"TV works fine, but I don't watch the news if I can help it. Why?"

"Well, darling," Billy said gleefully. "There is a big storm off the west coast coming this way, and unless the weatherman is wrong, we're fixin' to get at least nine to ten inches dumped on us this weekend. We didn't want to take a chance of getting caught in it on the road."

"You're kidding, right?"

"Well no, why would I do that? Turn on the tube and see."

Maggie jumped up nearly knocking Russell's beer over and pulled him up, and the two began to dance across the kitchen floor. Maggie's eyes were shining brightly when she exclaimed, "Oh, thank you, Lord, it's going to snow."

∽

Maggie couldn't sleep and spent much of the night watching the weather and staring out of the large window in the great room. The first flakes began to fall about two a.m., and by six o'clock, the front lawn and driveway were covered with a white blanket. She sipped cocoa and watched Russ as he pretended to be awake while lying with his head back in the big, comfortable chair. An occasional snore would send his head shooting up with an, "I'm awake, I promise, I'm awake."

Maggie finally had pity on him and told him to lie down on the sofa where she covered him with one of the Southwestern-patterned throws. Standing over him while watching him sleep, she thought he looked young and peaceful. His face had a morning beard with a couple of tiny scars on his forehead and a small imperfection on his nose. The cartilage was shifted slightly to one side as the result of a broken nose. He'd said his father was abusive. Maggie felt sorry for the little boy whose father had hurt him. She wanted to sit down and fold him in her arms, but she didn't because he wouldn't appreciate the gesture or the pity. He was still a very private man.

Was she falling in love with Russ? Her heart skipped, and her hand rested on her stomach. Her dreams had stopped, but she wasn't sure yet. She thought he needed to know, but she wasn't ready. He'd made her no promises. She didn't really know who or what he was, but he would tell her all about himself when he was ready. She could wait. And she could wait for the promises.

His eyes popped open and gave her a lazy smile. "Is it still snowing?"

"Yes, it hasn't let up all night. All the roads are snow packed, and the weather station is saying this is the biggest storm we've ever had this early."

Russ reached for her and brought her close for a kiss. "You're like a little kid. like Emma was on Christmas morning."

Maggie didn't want to say anything to dampen her jubilant mood, so she stood and walked toward the window. He followed her and put his arms around her pulling her against him.

"Emma was the reason I married Sarah. We had nothing in common except lust for each other. She was young, beautiful, and spoiled. She stroked my ego, and I was proud to show her off to my friends. That doesn't make for a long-lasting relationship. She wanted one thing; I wanted another. I wasn't surprised when she told me she was having an affair, but I never thought she would leave me and take Emma."

He turned her to face him and said, "You're very beautiful. Other than that, the two of you are nothing alike." He ran his finger down her face and rested it on her lips.

"You're the most independent woman I've ever met and by far the most accomplished."

"What are you talking about? I've got two years of college and a stint as an executive assistant in the mayor's office, which sounds so much more important than saying I was a secretary."

"Like Bella, you've got a lot of pride, and sometimes it can get in the way, but I wouldn't have you be any other way. You know I'm in love with you, Magdalena Morales, and you know that one of these days I've got to go home."

∼

THE STORM LASTED for two days, and the latest weather update indicated a record eleven inches. Russ and Billy were busy clearing the snow from the lodge and the gravel road leading to the main highway.

Maggie knocked the snow off her boots and left them on the porch when she entered the warm house. She found Bella dressed in wool slacks, a pretty turquoise sweater, and black boots. She was holding her purse.

"Where do you think you're going?"

"Well, smarty, anywhere I want to. I can still drive, but I would prefer that you drive me. I want you to take me into Taos. I have some business to do."

Maggie looked at Bella, opened her mouth to say more and then closed it. Bella would tell her what this was about when she was ready.

The temperature was hovering right above freezing when Maggie drove into the parking lot of the Centinel Bank. Bella was proud to say it was the oldest bank in the city, and she and Reggie were one of its first patrons.

Maggie cringed as she watched Bella make her way into the building while dodging melting puddles of snow and ice. Maggie could imagine Bella surviving being knocked down by thugs in her own yard and only suffering slight injuries, and then succumbing to a broken hip from a fall on the ice. What had Bella said not a week ago about pride?

She turned the car on and off and then on again while listening to a country station. Out of boredom, she counted all the customers as they came and went. She was up to twenty-five when she saw Bella walk out the front door carrying a small bag that businesses used for deposits. "What the heck?" Maggie wondered.

Bella put the pouch on Maggie's lap and said, "Here. Miguel's money after he died. I told the government I didn't want their damn money, but you know how they are. Reggie put it in a safe deposit box, and it's been there ever since. Why should we profit from our son's death?"

Maggie slid back the zipper and gasped when she saw stacks of hundred-dollar bills. "There must be …?

"Yes, thousands of dollars. We thought about giving it to the church, but I was mad at God. I let it sit for a while. And then when I forgave God, I decided He would tell me what to do with it. Now I know what to do. Save my family's history for my great-granddaughter. That would make Miguel happy."

CHAPTER 16

The howling wind in the trees might have unnerved a guest if there had actually been one in any of the cabins. Bella Morales was not a person who frightened easily. She had a past filled with clouds and sorrow yet balanced with enough sunshine to keep a soft smile on her lips. In her opinion, it was all about maintaining one's balance. Her husband had taught her that.

"What goes up, must come down," Reggie used to say. "While your balloons are floating in the air, enjoy them." It was his way of telling her to live in the moment, and his wisdom had helped guide her through her difficult, yet colorful life.

The loud banging on the door brought Bella's thoughts back to the present. At first, she thought it was the wind again, but she knew it was someone at the door. She took the shotgun down from the rack on the wall and pointed it at the door.

"Who's there. Say your name. I have a gun."

For a moment there was no sound, and then she heard

a man's voice. "Bella, it's me. It's Lyman. I mean you no harm."

Bella crossed to the room, opened the handle and kicked the door open. "You. Why are you here, Lyman O'Dell? This is my home, and you are not welcome."

He took a step forward, and she raised the gun to chest height. "Answer me."

Boney rose slowly from his bed by the fire and growled as Lyman tried to step into the house. The dog's ears were erect, and his high, bushy tail moved stiffly from side to side.

"I need to talk to you. Nobody else can help me. Please let me in."

Torn by conflicting emotions, her loyalty to Maggie caused her to hesitate. She had never warmed up to Lyman, but he did not frighten her.

"Please, Bella," he said.

She moved her hand down to silence Boney, and although he had ceased his aggressive behavior, he stood alert his eyes darting to Bella and back to the man.

She lowered the gun and stepped aside to let him enter. He moved into the room and stood close to the fire and far away from Boney. She took pity on him and motioned to the chair.

He sank into it, and his head fell into his hands for a moment before he raised his eyes to meet hers, and she saw the fear he could not hide.

"What is this about, Lyman? Have you come to give me bad news?" A flash of fear stabbed at her heart. "Is Maggie all right?"

"She's fine as far as I know. Where did she go tonight?"

"Not that it's any of your business, but she and Russell

went to town for supplies. They are working hard to get the cabins ready for the ski season. We are hoping to have many guests."

Lyman looked confused. "I don't get it. I thought Cielo Verde was losing money."

"It is, but things are getting better."

"Why? What happened?"

"Well, the big snowstorm for one thing. We haven't had this much powder in many years, and Russell is a magician on the computer. He updated our website, and he said he's been tweeting, whatever that means, and posting things all over the Internet. We're taking reservations on the computer now, and business is finally picking up. Having more money than we thought we did, didn't hurt."

"What money? Where did you get more money?"

"I don't have to tell you that. Why are you asking so many questions?"

Lyman's laugh was bitter. "I only want what's best for you and Maggie."

"Since when? What is wrong with you? You are talking in riddles. I can see the fear in your eyes."

"That's because you could always read me like a book. Gave me the creeps when I was married to Maggie, but now, I need your powers to get me out of a jam."

"Tell me what you came to say. You are making an old woman tired."

"I'm frightened, Bella. I made a deal with the devil, and I want you to read those cards and tell me if I am going to get out of this mess alive."

When Maggie and Russell got back to the lodge, they saw Lyman's Range Rover in the yard in front of the house.

"What is he doing here?" Russell said.

"I'm not sure, but I'm going to find out." She quickly made her way up the steps and burst into the room where Lyman and Bella sat at the dining room table. It appeared that Bella had recently completed a reading, and Lyman did not look well.

"What's going on here?" Maggie said. "Why are you bothering Bella?"

"Now hold on there, Mags. I'm …"

"Do not call me Mags, and do not tell me to hold on. I want you to leave this house immediately."

Lyman stood and paced. "I came to see Bella because I didn't know what else to do. I've got myself in a real mess, and I need help."

"What are you saying? What kind of a mess?"

"I'm saying that I am begging you to sell your land. You're going to lose it to the county anyway, so why not sell it and make some money?"

Maggie ran her fingers through her hair. "Who says I'm not making any money? Since when do you dare to offer me advice?"

He put his hand on her arm. "I'll always be around to …"

"Actually, you won't," Russell said as he pushed Lyman away from Magdalena. Lyman ended up off balance and against the wall. His eyes flashed with outrage. Then he opened the door and bellowed as he ran out into the yard with Boney barking and nipping at his heels.

"You'll get yours, Murphy. I know all about you."

"Get back," Russell said. "I think he's dangerous."

Maggie moved toward the window and started to disagree, but then she saw Lyman waving a gun in the air as he made his way to his car.

"You have to sell this place," he yelled. "It's the only chance I have. If you ever loved me, Maggie, you have to help me now. They're going to kill me."

"What is he talking about?" Russell said.

Maggie looked confused. "I honestly have no idea."

∽

BY THE TIME Lyman drove back into town, his racing pulse had calmed somewhat. Following Bella's advice, he began to take deep breaths, count to four, exhale, and repeat. At least he wasn't close to hyperventilating anymore. The old woman hadn't given him any of the answers he needed. Instead, she spouted stupid moral platitudes about greed hurting him and his need to change his attitudes or he could be severely injured. She'd said he was an unhappy man that only took and never gave. He hadn't gone to her to get a review of his character. He needed her to give him answers on how to get out of his mess. He left the gun under the seat, parked the Range Rover in front of his house, and made his way inside.

He planned on having a hot cup of coffee and a shower before he tried to figure out what to do next, but he never got the chance. Two men emerged from the shadows in the hallway, and before he could react, they dragged him into the bathroom and shoved his head into the open toilet. He screamed and clawed, but he was helpless. There were two of them, and they were muscle-bound and determined. He was going to die, to drown, right here in his own bathroom in a filthy toilet bowl. Each time he managed to move his head enough to suck in a little air he was forcefully plunged back under the water. When he thought his lungs would burst, they pulled him up and threw him onto the bed and hogtied him. He coughed and gasped while trying to pull in air through his mouth as water poured out of his nose.

"You've got real pretty, manicured hands here, Lyman," one of the men said, gently rubbing his fingers before he snapped the middle finger back. The pain was excruciating, and tears filled Lyman's eyes.

"What do you want? Why are you doing this?"

"O'Dell, you know what we want," the other man said grasping Lyman's hand and forcing it down flat on the nightstand. He picked up the brass lamp and slammed it against Lyman's knuckles.

"Oh, my God … oh, my God," Lyman wheezed and then stammered, "I'll give you whatever you want. Please don't hurt me anymore."

"Jaime here wanted to cut off your ear, but I said no, cause we're not animals, but Jaime, he's pretty hard to control. If we have to come back again, I don't know if I can stop him. Since he didn't get to play very long tonight, he may decide to take that aristocratic nose too."

Lyman began to tremble and sob. "Please, what can I do?"

"Make the right decision, O'Dell. We're here to deliver a message."

Lyman stayed silent and hoped they wouldn't notice the tremble in his voice.

"We've come to tell you time's up, and the deal's off."

Lyman coughed. "What's that supposed to mean?"

"It means you screwed around too long and now your ex has found a way to get herself out of trouble. She doesn't need to sell her land anymore."

"How do you know that?" he said. His surprise was genuine.

"The boss makes it his business to know. Your days are numbered. Better make them count. Find another way to pay your debt, or you'll end up a cold stiff in a pine box with a bunch of your parts missing. This will be your last warning."

∼

LYMAN WAITED until there had been no sounds in the house for several minutes before he got up. With much difficulty, he made his way into the kitchen and managed to loosen the cords around his wrists.

He struggled to make his way to the car and then drove slowly toward town. By the time he got to the bank, he could barely put one foot in front of the other. His stomach churned, he was shaking, and his hand was throbbing. He could see it was broken. He needed to see a doctor, but he was too afraid to go to the ER. What if they found him? He needed to get away. As far away from Angel Falls and New Mexico as he could. Make them think he was dead and then hide until everything blew over. It wasn't that far to Mexico. If he left now, he could be there by tomorrow afternoon.

He opened the vault and took out stacks of big bills and crammed them into one of the suitcases he hadn't filled with clothes. The police would be looking for him first thing Monday morning, but by then he would be safe and sitting on the beach drinking a Margarita.

After rummaging around in his desk at the office, he found a yellow, legal pad and a pen. It took him nearly thirty minutes of trial and error and lots of scratch-outs to compose the note he planned to leave for Bella and Maggie.

If he had ever loved anyone, it would have been Maggie. She was sweet and beautiful. Why couldn't things have worked out? If she had forgiven him, they would still be together, and he wouldn't be in the trouble he was in. He could have convinced her to get Bella to sell. The note would be perfect. Everyone would think he had taken his own life. He would be safe, and although not living the life he wanted, at least he would be living.

He left the note under a framed photo of Magdalena and him on their wedding day. It had been there for years. Then, he closed his office and walked out the front door.

He had traveled only fourteen miles when his car sputtered and then stopped. Realizing that for several days he had forgotten all about getting gas, he coasted to the side of the road. Before he could formulate a plan, he saw a dark sedan pull up behind him. Two men in khaki pants and blue vests made their way up behind his car.

"Step out of the car, sir, and keep your hands where we can see them."

"Who are you?" he said.

"We are ATF agents, Bentley and Moss. We're taking you into the State Police office to answer a few questions about the fire at Bella Morales' place."

Lyman did as he was told, and with shaking knees stood and faced the car so they could search him. He was filled with relief and gratitude that he was in the hands of the law, and not the mob boss who had threatened to kill him.

"You appear to be injured, Mr. O'Dell. We followed you from your house and then to the bank. Are you leaving town, sir?"

"Uh, no. I'm driving into Taos to the hospital. I slammed my hand in the car door."

Bentley opened the car door and turned and nodded to the other agent. "Looks like you packed for a long stay at the hospital. Three suitcases."

"I have a vacation planned. California. For a conference," he said.

"I have a gun under the front seat," he said. "It's not loaded. I don't know why you want to talk to me. I don't know anything about the fire at the Morales' place, and I really need to get to the ER to get my hand X-rayed. I think it may be broken."

"We'll be more than happy to take you there, and we can talk afterward."

"But I really don't have the time … you see … I really need to catch my flight, you know, to California."

"I'm sure that won't be a problem, Mr. O'Dell."

"Listen, it's not me you need to be talking with. I don't know anything about a fire, but I'm sure the man staying out at the lodge does. I can tell you all about him."

"That's very interesting, sir," Agent Bentley said as he helped Lyman into the backseat of the car.

CHAPTER 17

The morning light flooded the bedroom as dust motes swirled around in the air. Maggie made a mental note to make sure to give the room a thorough dusting and vacuuming before the end of the day. She had been busy working with Russ to ready the cabins before the winter ski season began, and she had neglected the housekeeping chores in the big house. Fortunately, there would be a cleaning crew once the season got underway, and she would not have to do everything by herself.

Maggie rolled to her left and stretched out her arm to find the other side of the bed cold and empty. She had fallen asleep with Russ's warm, muscular body close beside her, and she felt a twinge of disappointment that he had gone upstairs. She felt his gallant gesture to protect her grandmother's sensibilities was noble, but unnecessary. Bella was not easily offended, nor was she oblivious to the romantic activities taking place in her house. Maggie chose to believe that she had Bella's blessing.

She made up the bed, put on a fluffy robe, and crossed

the hall to the bathroom. After brushing her teeth and taking a hot, invigorating shower, she combed out her long black hair and dried it. Looking into the mirror, she stroked mascara on her thick eyelashes, added a touch of lip gloss to her generous lips, smacked them together and started her day.

She was having a hard time wrapping her head around Lyman's bizarre behavior last night. Bella said he was irrational and thought someone was going to kill him. She wasn't forthcoming about what she told him after reading the cards. Bella considered a reading to be as confidential as speaking to a minister or a psychologist. Even if she loathed the person, she didn't reveal what the cards had foretold about him.

Maggie heard dishes clinking in the kitchen, and she wondered if Bella had awakened early and wanted her breakfast. She found Russell wearing one of her aprons while standing at the stove with a spatula in his hand. She could smell bacon and something else she could not identify.

"What's that delicious fragrance?" she said.

"Banana pancakes."

"Since when do you know how to make those?"

"I saw some bananas that were getting too ripe and found some Bisquick in the pantry. Anybody can add milk to Bisquick and mash bananas. Even me. I used to make them all the time for Emma."

His crystal-blue eyes misted, and Maggie held her breath and waited to see if he would fall apart, but he held it together. She had no idea whether she should continue talking about the child or change the subject, so she said nothing at all. She walked up behind him and put her arms around him and held on tight.

He didn't move for a minute and then turned away from the stove and pulled her close. "I hated to leave you last night."

"Don't get me started," she said. "We are never going to agree about this issue."

"What issue?" Bella said as she entered the room. She looked rested and healthy again, even though she still walked gingerly moving her feet slowly.

Russell gave Maggie a momentary look of discomfort, but she ignored him. "You're better off not knowing," Maggie said.

Bella grinned mischievously and sat down at the table. "How long until breakfast is ready?"

"How about right now?" Russell said and began to fill a plate.

They each had one serving of pancakes and honey served with a side of crisp bacon, and Maggie was considering a second helping when Boney's sharp, piercing barks shattered the morning calm. He only barked when necessary, and they all knew it. Three anxious faces turned toward the window.

Russell stood up and made his way to the door. He opened it and saw two dark SUVs speeding up the road toward the house.

"Who's coming?" Bella said.

"I'm not sure," Russell said. "It looks like the law."

A short time later, the cars stopped, and both front doors opened on one of them. Two burly men wearing khakis, blue shirts and ball caps with the yellow letters

ATF prominently displayed, exited the car and slammed the doors shut. No one got out of the second car.

Russell knew who they were. He had endured hours of questions after the fire at his house all those months ago.

"Who is it, Russell?" Bella said.

"ATF agents. Maybe they have some information about the fire in the barn." He met them at the door and opened the screen. "Gentlemen, may we help you?"

"Maybe we should do this inside," the taller man said.

"Sure. Come on in."

The agent looked at Bella and Maggie. He tipped his hat and then put it back on. "Ladies, good morning. Sorry to interrupt your breakfast."

"What's this about?" Maggie said.

"We have a few questions to ask Mr. Zarek about the fire."

"There's no one here by that name," Maggie said.

Russell's face lost all its color, and he looked into Maggie's curious eyes. "I'm sorry, Maggie. That is my name. It's me they want to talk to," Russell said.

"What is this about?" Bella said. "We've already answered all your questions about the fire on our property. You are mistaken. Russell had nothing to do with it. He was out with my granddaughter that night."

"This is concerning a different issue, ma'am. I'm sorry we had to disturb you."

Maggie had not said a word and sat immobilized in her chair with a look of confusion in her black eyes.

"We need to take you with us to Albuquerque to answer some questions about the explosion and fire at your house, and subsequently the murder of your wife and child," the agent said. "You can get in the car and come voluntarily, or we can arrest you and hold you for questioning for seventy-two hours. Your choice."

"I don't understand. They died in an accidental fire, a malfunction of the furnace," Russell insisted.

"The fire was not an accident, Mr. Zarek. Their deaths have been ruled as homicides."

Russell's jaw tightened, and he took a step forward and grasped the back of a chair.

"Well, Zarek. What will it be?"

Russell hesitated a moment and then nodded and walked down the steps to the waiting car with an agent on both sides of him, his face a mask of confusion. As he got into the back of the car, he looked toward the house, but no one had followed him outside.

∼

Maggie finally understood the full meaning of being in shock. She felt as if she had been given an injection of Novocain. She felt nothing. No anger. No sorrow.

"Are you okay, mija?" Bella said. "Your face has no color. Sit there. Be still," she ordered. "I will get you something that will help." She opened one of the high cabinets and stretched until she could reach the bottle of mescal she kept for emergencies. This was the strong kind with a worm in the bottle. She poured it into a shot glass and placed it in front of Maggie. "Drink this," she insisted.

Maggie downed the shot, swallowed and coughed. "Oh, Bella. That's awful," she said.

"Got your color back for sure," Bella said. "Now, let's talk about this."

"What is there to say? I don't even know the man who

just left here. He's been lying to me for weeks. He didn't even give me his real name."

"Ah, yes, but why not? What was his reason?"

"How would I know?" Maggie said. She was trying not to raise her voice to Bella, but her anguish was almost overcoming her control.

"Maybe he was trying to protect you," Bella said.

Maggie looked at her through tear-filled eyes but did not respond.

"Do you think this man loves you?" she said.

Maggie did not answer her. She considered pouring herself another shot but decided against it.

"Do you love him?" Bella persisted.

Maggie put her hand on her heart as if testing it to see if it was still beating. "God help me, Bella. I still do."

"Then, you must give him a chance to explain. After you hear his reasons, you can decide if you believe him, and if you can accept what he has done."

Maggie's tears spilled down her cheeks. "I'm not sure I have the courage to find out."

"Well, I do. I have courage for both of us. Now stand up. Go pack a bag. Then go ask Mrs. Hansen to care for Boney and keep her eye on the place while we are gone."

"Gone? Where?"

"To Albuquerque. To the place they took Russell. We have questions, too, and he's the only one with the answers. Hurry, dear child. Russell needs our help. We have to go."

~

MAGGIE WALKED like a zombie toward the storage unit for the winter gear for guests. She found Billy and Dora cleaning skis and snowboards. Dora stopped scrubbing when Maggie walked in. "Good Lord, girl, you look like you've seen a ghost? Are you all right? Is Bella?"

Billy walked over to her and said, "Does it have anything to do with those big black cars that were parked in front of the house?"

"Yes, I ..." Looking around, Maggie saw a bench and said, "I have to sit down." She took a deep breath and exhaled. "Those men were from the ATF in Albuquerque. They came for Russell."

"What do you mean came for Russell?"

"They think he ..." she squeezed her eyes shut and finally said, "they think he killed his family. Oh, my God. They think he murdered them." Tears choked her as Dora pulled Maggie into her arms.

"Hush, girl. It will be all right."

"It's got to be a mistake. Don't it?" said Billy. "He's from Albuquerque. What did he do there?"

"I haven't asked him, but I know he owns a company, something with computers, and I guess he has plenty of money."

"Well, I'll be damned," Billy said. "Pardon my French, Miss Maggie. I knew he looked familiar. He was on the cover of one of my bike magazines. He's a big Harley collector. Rich son of a gun, but his name wasn't Murphy, it was ..."

"Zarek, his name is Russell Zarek," Maggie said.

PART II

CHAPTER 18

Maggie pulled out of the Rio Grande Visitor Center lot where they'd stopped for a quick break, tapped her fingers on the steering wheel of the truck, turned toward Bella, and said, "It appears we've encountered the stones in the road that the cards predicted, but they look more like boulders to me."

"The cards also told you something else. Do you remember?"

"Yes, something about working together to overcome those obstacles."

"Well?" Bella said sounding frustrated.

"The man I love is in jail for murdering his wife and his daughter. How can working together fix that?"

"You don't even know his story. You didn't ask," Bella said, disappointment in her voice. "Russell is a good man. You will see."

"I asked plenty of times. He didn't tell me."

"Maybe you never asked the right questions."

"What is that supposed to mean?"

"Did you ever ask Russell how he got so much money, or where he worked?"

"Well, I did ask him if he'd robbed a bank."

"Hmm," Bella snorted.

"No, he's private. I didn't want to intrude"

"You sleep with a man, but you can't intrude by asking a simple question? I don't think you wanted to know. I think you wanted to play at life without any of the consequences."

"I don't know what you're talking about."

"Oh, yes you do, Magdalena Consuela." Bella turned her head away and said, "I'm taking a nap."

"That's what you always say when you don't like where a conversation is going, or you don't get your way." Maggie looked at Bella, but she knew the conversation was over. It was Bella's way of telling her if she loved Russell, she should trust him.

She had loved Lyman and look where that got her. Well, okay, in truth she had to admit he wasn't the love of her life, and she had never trusted him. He was rich, handsome, and handy, and she was lonely and grieving for her mother.

Before they left the house, Maggie had googled Russell Zarek. It seems he had lied by omission. His name was Russell Murphy Zarek, and he was the owner of Zarek International along with his partner Darren Hess. Maggie gulped when she read that Russell was worth close to two hundred million dollars. Yes, she thought, he definitely had the money to give her a loan.

There was a brief article about his marriage to Sarah Tillis, a young debutant from Texas, but that's all there was about his private life. Maggie thought Russell's wife was everything she was not. The picture in the story showed a tall, model-slim woman with pale blonde hair and cool blue eyes. She had smooth skin, a small nose and chin, and wide-set eyes. She appeared to be much younger than her husband.

Then, she saw the picture on the magazine cover that Billy had seen. It was a caption of Russ standing in front of a vintage Harley he had donated to a charity organization that supported homes for abused women and their children.

He had told her no lies, but he had not told the whole truth. Because of his background, Russell had issues with trust. That was something they both could work on. She wanted to see him, and she needed to let him know that she believed in him.

Maggie splurged on a suite at the hotel, so that she and Bella could have separate bedrooms. The living room was large, and the air freshener smelled pleasant and clean. As soon as she got Bella settled on the sofa and gave her a cold glass of water, she quickly called Roddy to let him know why they were in town.

"What do you mean Russell is in jail?" His voice was rough with anxiety.

"They think he is responsible for the death of his wife and daughter. They died in a fire last year."

"Here in Albuquerque?"

"Yes. His real name is Russell Zarek."

"I know that name. Rich weirdo."

"Weirdo? Why would you say that? Russell's not weird. You've met him."

"I don't know. Maybe because he shuns publicity, doesn't like the limelight, and comes down the mountain after an extended walkabout." His words were loaded with ridicule.

"And those are the reasons you have for calling him weird?" She sounded annoyed.

"If I had all of his money, Mags, I think I would have to flaunt it a little bit."

Maggie clutched the phone tightly while waiting until he finally said, "I remember that fire, but there hasn't been much talk about it since. So now they think he did it, huh? I guess you don't ever really know a person."

"He didn't do it, Roddy. He loved his daughter. He couldn't have killed her."

"Come on, Mags, you hardly know the guy. Believe me. I've seen and represented some expert liars. Just because your dog likes him, doesn't mean he's a nice guy. Lots of my clients have dogs."

"You don't have to believe him, Roddy. I'm asking you to represent him as a favor to Bella and me. She's here with me, and she's worried and upset."

"Bella's on his side? Did I hear you right?" He sighed, and his tone changed and lost its steely edge. "Okay, Mags, I'm in. I'm on a brief break from court which means I can't do anything right now. I'll have my secretary call and find out where they're holding him, and she'll call you with the information. Tell me where you're staying, and she'll get in touch."

~

RUSSELL SAT on a cot with a threadbare mattress in a large holding cell. At present, he was the only occupant. A lidless toilet sat against the far wall. Maggie could smell the lingering odor of Lysol, stale urine, and the unwashed bodies who had previously occupied this dark, desolate place.

Russell pushed aside the untamed shock of hair that had grown too long on his brow, and his worried eyes sought Maggie's. "I told the police my brother Hugh said I was with him that night. Like I said before, I don't remember. I was upset about losing Emma, and I had too much to drink. Believe me, I'm kicking myself for it. That's not something I usually do. I need Hugh to corroborate my story, but first I have to let him know what's going on. Will you call him and fill him in?"

"You know I will," she said. She handed him her phone. "Put his number in here, and I'll call him as soon as I get back to the hotel."

"I don't know his number. It's in my phone contacts, but I don't have any idea where my phone is. I lost it that night at the bar. My brother's name is Hugh Powell. Call my associate at the office. She'll give it to you."

"What's that number?"

Russell looked sheepishly at her. "I can't remember."

"No problem, I'll google it." A probing query came into her eyes. "Russell, why didn't you tell me who you were? I guess I can understand what stopped you when we first met, but after we became close?" Her words rang in the silent room almost an accusation of his duplicity. "You didn't trust me," Maggie said. It wasn't a question but a statement of fact.

"It wasn't a matter of trust. People know who I am, and some pretend to like me for that. For what I can do for them. It was easier to keep my guard up until I got to know you and Bella."

Maggie's temper flared, but she tapped it back down and tried to listen without judging. She'd never had his kind of money, and she guessed she might feel the same way.

"Then, I was sort of stuck. I tried to tell you when I offered to help you and Bella keep the lodge afloat. I would have told you; I promise. There never seemed to be the right time."

"Did you know when you left home that you were a suspect in their murders?"

"No, I had no idea. The fire was an accident. It had to be. No one would want to hurt Emma. She was such a sweet little girl," he said as anguish encompassed his face.

He gently touched her cheek and said, "Magdalena, I didn't do it. I would never have hurt them. Sarah was a spoiled young woman, but she didn't deserve to die. And you've got to know that I would never hurt my own baby girl. I couldn't. I wouldn't."

Tears filled Maggie's eyes. She took his hands in hers. "It's a terrible tragedy, Russ. I believe you. Hugh will come in, tell the police you were with him, and they will have to let you go."

"But if they were murdered, I can't understand why?"

"You said Sarah told you she was having an affair. Maybe it was that guy, or a jealous wife, or lover? Oh jeez, I don't know. That sounds like a line from a movie. I can't imagine."

Russell pressed his forehead to hers and whispered, "I love you, Magdalena. Thank you for coming and thanks for asking Roddy to represent me."

"I love you too, Russ. We will get through this

together. Bella assures me everything will turn out the way it should."

"Well, if Bella says so," he said smiling for the first time.

"I'll find the number for your company and call. Who should I ask for?"

"Olive Greeley. She's a sweet gal and will give you any information you think will help."

She squeezed his hand. "Is the phone call to Hugh all you need? Can I bring you anything?"

His laugh was bitter and sharp. "Like what? A file in a cake?"

~

Olive Greeley pushed open the office door without knocking, "Darren," she said with excitement ringing in her voice, "some woman called me and ask for Hugh Powell's number."

Darren Hess glanced up with a bored expression on his face and said, "Okay, give it to her. What's the big deal?"

"The big deal is that Russell told her to call me. Russell. He's back in town. Isn't that terrific?"

"Where is he and where the hell has he been?" Darren said.

"She didn't say, and when I asked her who she was, she said she was a friend of Russell's, and he asked her to call me. What do you think?"

"I think you need to call Hugh and see what's going on. Russell needs to get his ass back here before the whole company falls apart."

CHAPTER 19

Hugh Powell agreed to come to the hotel as soon as Maggie let him know what the situation was, and he knocked on the door about forty-five minutes later. Maggie let him in, and her first thought was that he looked nothing like Russ. Hugh was a shorter, leaner version of his brother with darker hair and brown eyes. Their faces were not the same at all. In a GQ Magazine-cover fashion, he was attractive, but his good looks did not work any magic on her.

"It's nice to meet you, Hugh. I'm Magdalena Morales. I want to introduce my great-grandmother, Bella Morales. Bella, this is Hugh Powell, Russell's brother."

"I'm happy to know you both," he said. "Although I'm not sure what's going on or how the two of you are acquainted with Russ. He is my stepbrother, and I haven't heard from him in months. Haven't seen him since the funeral. He wouldn't take any of my calls, and the next thing I know, he's in jail."

Maggie motioned toward the dark blue sofa near the window. "Please sit down."

Hugh moved the colorful throw pillows aside and arranged himself on the couch. "I'd like to know what's going on," he said.

"That's why you're here," Maggie said. "Russell wanted me to fill you in on the events leading up to this terrible mistake." Maggie's phone rang, and she reached for it and answered. Hugh and Bella could hear her end of the conversation and saw her nodding her head. "Yes, I know," she said. "He's just arrived, and we were going to …" She looked at Hugh and then continued. "Well, okay, if you think that's best. Sure. We are in room 521 at the Hyatt Regency."

She cleared her throat and turned toward Hugh. "That was Roddy Eastman. He's Russell's attorney, and he's asked me to wait until he gets here to listen to your story. If you don't mind, we can have some coffee and wait for him. He won't be long. He's leaving the jail now."

Hugh's eyes narrowed and hardened. "Why does he need to be here?"

"If you are going to be the alibi for Russell, every word you say will be important. Mr. Eastman wants to hear it for himself rather than second-hand from me."

"Fine," Hugh said. "But in the meantime, can we sit here quietly and drink our coffee? I'm not big on chit-chat."

The silence grew tight with tension. Bella studied him thoughtfully for a few moments. "*Qué grosero*," she muttered.

"Pardon?" Hugh said.

"That's fine," Bella said. "I'm not much of a talker myself."

Maggie worked to suppress a smile.

~

HUGH FELT like he was in some surreal nightmare. Ever since Russell took off without a word, he had been wondering when he would be compelled to confess to all the betrayals, lies, and misrepresentations in which he had been involved. He often pondered how he had fallen into such a shameful trap.

Looking back, he was sure it had all started years ago when Russell invited him to Emma's birthday party. He remembered going to the house as Russell's little brother and leaving several hours later as a full-grown man who had a bad case of the hots for Russell's wife Sarah.

It wasn't anything Sarah said, but it was the way she walked, the way she smiled, the way she leaned in close to him, and the alluring fragrance of her perfume. Sarah was closer to his age than to Russell's, and he could see that his brother, nearly a decade older than his wife, had stability and maturity to offer her, but his personality was short on excitement and adventure.

In retrospect, he knew he should have declined their generous offer to live with them and occupy their guest room. But he was nearly broke, and the offer of a job in Russell's warehouse and free room and board was too good to resist.

His original plan was to get his life back on track and save enough of his salary to get his own place. He was determined to avoid spending any time alone with Sarah and discarded the notion that he would ever step over the line.

As time went on, even though Hugh had tried to resist because he loved his brother and did not want to hurt him, Sarah's charms were too much to resist. They spent as many hours in bed as they could, and they tried to stay away from each other when Russell was around. Hugh made it a point to be too busy or to be out of town for holiday celebrations. He didn't want Russell to notice any familiar behaviors between Sarah and him.

It had gone on that way for over a year, and Hugh remembered that Sarah thought the arrangement was working out well for everyone. He was of a different opinion and had reached the point in his life where he wanted to be up-front with his brother and stop sneaking around.

"I want you to tell Russell about us and ask him for a divorce. We can't keep doing this forever, and I want you to marry me."

She had looked at him as if he were crazy. "You want me to give up my home, my husband, and his money, for you?" Her mouth twitched with amusement.

He put his hands on her arms and said, "That's exactly what I want, Sarah. If you don't tell Russell, then I will. This secret relationship has to end."

"Oh, Hugh, hon, you're serious, aren't you?" She flipped her long blonde hair over her shoulders and stepped back. "We don't have a relationship. We have sex. Nice sex but still just sex, and the sneaking around makes it much more exciting."

"Why are you doing this?" Hugh said. "You love me; I love you. When you divorce Russell, you'll get a ton of money, and we don't have to stay here. We can move anywhere you want."

"Oh, I know that and especially with Emma as a big bargaining chip."

Hugh was crushed and grabbed her forcefully by the arms. "You can't do this to me."

"Let go," she said. She raked her fingernails across his face and then slapped him. "You get the hell out of my house," she said. "You are going to ruin everything. Russell is the one who owns Zarek International. I'm leaving him all right, but not for you. You're just a flunky who works in the warehouse. But as a parting gift, I'll make sure Russell knows everything about us and what a great stud you are."

He could still hear the echo of her laugh.

∽

REMEMBERING that night from over six months ago had given him a headache, and he turned to Maggie and Bella with an apologetic smile. "I'm sorry if I came across as a jerk. The truth is I have a killer headache. Any chance you have aspirin or Tylenol?"

Maggie crossed the room and found her purse on the round, glass table under a pile of coats and scarves. After a few moments, she unzipped a pink, makeup bag and removed a small, white bottle. "Here," she said, "you dig one of these out, and I'll get you some water."

He opened the container and shook two white capsules into his hand. Maggie took a water bottle from the small refrigerator and handed it to him. After he popped the pills into his mouth, he gulped down the water and swallowed. She could see his Adam's apple bob up and down twice.

After a few more minutes of an awkward silence during which Bella did not offer any sympathy or a gracious acceptance of his apology, they heard a double tap on the door. Maggie peered through the peephole and then slid off the chain and let Roddy in.

Introductions were made quickly, and the two men shook hands. Roddy wasted no time in getting to the point.

"Russell told me that he was with you the night that his wife and child died in the explosion," Roddy said. "Can you confirm that?"

"It's true. We were at a bar having a few beers together."

"Which bar?"

"We went to The Thirsty Lizard on Academy Road."

"Did anybody see you there?"

Hugh bristled at the question. "Like who?"

"Like, someone who could confirm your story?"

"Well, I guess so. If she still works there, the waitress knows me. I've been there lots of times." Roddy took out a small leather notebook from his pocket. "Name?"

Hugh thought for a while. "Well, it was Tara or Scarlett. Something from *Gone with the Wind*, if I remember right. We didn't talk to her much. We would signal for more beer and the check. You don't need a lot of words if the waitress is good. She's got her eyes on you the whole time."

"What did you and Russell talk about?" Roddy said.

"He was really down and out. He said that Sarah had told him she wanted a divorce, and she was going after full custody of Emma. We're not that close, but I ran into him at the office, and he looked upset, so I invited him for a drink."

Bella shifted in her chair and locked her eyes on Hugh. "Did Russell know that you were sleeping with his wife? Was that the reason for the divorce?" Bella said.

Maggie cast a look of surprise at her great-grandmother and nearly choked. "Bella ... for heaven's sake," she said.

Hugh brushed off Bella's words and did not attempt to deny her accusation. "Oh, hell no," Hugh said, and amusement flickered in his eyes. "Sarah already had another guy on the hook by that time. I didn't make enough money to keep her happy."

"Did you confess to your brother about your affair with his wife?" Roddy said. His question was matter-of-fact as if what he learned had already occurred to him.

"I wanted to. I was going to but ..." He rose from his seat as if propelled by an explosive force and began to pace. He didn't look at any of them. Then he stopped and turned to face Roddy. "Would you? Would you kick a man when he's down?"

He paused, and his eyes darted back and forth between them, but no one answered his questions.

"I don't think splitting with Sarah was bothering him too much," he continued, " but he was a complete mess because he thought he might lose Emma. He loved that baby girl so much. There's no way I was going to tell him that I'd been having sex with Sarah. Not that night anyway."

Roddy nodded noncommittally. "I see. Can you

confirm the hours that you two were together and what time Russell went home?"

"We were there from about nine o'clock until the bar closed at two a.m. Then we went to Waffle House for coffee and a bite to eat. Russell got a message on his phone from his house about three-fifteen letting him know there was a fire."

"You mean his wife sent a text?" Maggie asked.

"Nah, he's got one of those smart houses. The app controls everything. The app would have automatically notified the fire department, too. We took a taxi out there because neither of us was fit to drive."

Hugh rubbed his head and his eyes. Maggie was pretty sure he was still suffering from the effects of having had too much to drink the night before.

"You know, it's funny," Hugh said. "Well, I guess not funny since the results were so drastic, but Russell told me Sarah wasn't there that night. She was moving to some hotel until the divorce was settled, and that's why he agreed to go to the bar with me. He didn't want to go home to an empty house. Normally he'd have been there holed up in his office."

"Well, this could be helpful information, Hugh. Thank you. I am going to the bar to get a statement from the waitress if possible. The best way to help Russell is to tell the police everything you have told me. Be truthful and don't leave anything out. If you lie about even one little thing, they could throw out your whole statement. I will get in touch with the authorities tonight and arrange for us to meet with them. We want to get Russ out of that cell as soon as possible."

Roddy stood and gave both Bella and Maggie gentle

hugs. He shook Hugh's hand and turned to leave. After he had opened the door, he turned back to say, "And stay away from the jail and from Russell until the police have taken your formal statement. We don't want them to think you and your brother made up a convenient story."

"I get it," Hugh said.

CHAPTER 20

A stocky man of medium height walked into the interview room and introduced himself to Roddy. "I'm Agent Matt Bentley of the Alcohol Tobacco and Firearms Department. I see you've already met Detective Flores. Mr. Zarek and I have already met. Or should I call you Mr. Murphy?"

Roddy stuck out his hand and said, "I'm Roddy Eastman, Mr. Zarek's attorney, and my client did not break any laws by not giving you his full name. He wasn't a suspect in the fire at the Morales' home, and he was with Mrs. Morales' great-granddaughter at the time. He also did not know that the authorities were looking for him to question him about the death of his family."

"Yes, it seems, Mr. Zarek is very fortunate with his alibis." Bentley placed a legal pad on the table and took out a pen from his suit jacket. He turned to look at Russell. "I wanted to discuss a few details about your wife's murder before I turn this investigation over to the local authorities."

He gave Russell a half-smile and said, "But before I do that, my partner and I had a very lengthy conversation with Lyman O'Dell the night before last. He didn't seem to be very fond of you and expressed his belief that you were responsible for the fire at his ex-wife's home. Since that fire is an ongoing investigation, I'm not at liberty to discuss anything about that case with you, but I would like to assure you the bureau is not looking at you as a suspect."

"May I ask one question?" Russell said.

"You may ask. I may not be able to answer."

"Are Maggie and Bella still in danger of any additional trouble?"

"From what I understand at this time, the two Morales ladies should have nothing further to worry about."

Russell was noticeably relieved as he said, "Thank you, I appreciate your candor."

"As to this case, your late wife, Sarah Zarek, did not die from smoke inhalation as was first believed. Nor did she die from anything related to the fire. She died from blunt force trauma to the head."

Russell was momentarily speechless in his surprise. Then, although he didn't want to know, he had to ask. "And Emma?"

"The medical examiner has ruled her cause of death to be smoke inhalation. She was asleep, and it appears she was unaware of the fire."

Tears pooled in Russell's eyes as he looked away from Bentley and said, "Did she feel any pain?"

"It seems unlikely that she did. Her death appeared peaceful."

"And Sarah?"

"Her body was found in the living room close to the origin of the fire. There was significant damage caused by the flames and heat that made the original determination of an accidental death plausible. It was later that her death was ruled a homicide."

Bentley stood and looked directly at Russell, "That being said, I will no longer be an active participant in the investigation of your wife's and daughter's deaths. I sincerely hope, Mr. Zarek, that the guilty party can be swiftly brought to justice."

Russell watched Bentley walk out of the room but was too numb even to acknowledge his exit. The fire was not accidental, and someone had murdered Sarah. The fire was only a convenient way of covering up a crime, and his precious daughter had merely been collateral damage.

Detective Flores took a sip of coffee out of a mug with an American flag and a blue line running across the bottom. "Would you gentlemen care for a cup? It's not bad. I have my own machine. Stuff in the break room tastes like acid."

Roddy answered for both of them with a polite, "No, thank you."

"Okay then, we'll get started."

"Mr. Zarek is speaking with you as a courtesy, and as you know, is under no obligation to do so," Roddy explained.

"Yes, and I appreciate his cooperation." The detective cleared his throat and said, "Mr. Zarek, what is a smart home?"

Caught off balance, Russell didn't know what to say? Why was he asking? "It's a home that is connected to a device that enables remote monitoring."

"That sounds pretty complicated. Can you break it down a little?"

"Sure, basically any device connected to the Internet can communicate with a computer or phone if it has the necessary application. If you forget to turn off the coffee machine, or if you're not sure, you can remotely check. You can also set your alarm system, set up security cameras," he opened his arms wide, "the list is endless."

"Well, now that sounds a little too Sci-Fi for me. Tell me, can the app control the heating system or the water heater?"

"Yes, if those appliances are equipped with smart thermostats."

"Do you have a smart home, Mr. Zarek?"

"Where are you going with this?" Roddy interrupted. "What would my client having a smart home have to do with anything?"

"All I'm trying to do is gather information. Is your company involved with this technological marvel?"

"I think you know it is, Detective, or you wouldn't be asking. My company developed software for these systems, and my home is a prototype as well as my partner's home and those of several others at the company."

"I think we are going to stop this interview right here," Roddy said. "I was of an understanding that Mr. Zarek was no longer a suspect since his stepbrother provided an established alibi. It looks like you are trying to follow the same direction on a different avenue. Let's go, Russell."

Before Roddy could get him out of the room, Russell blurted, "I did not kill my wife or my daughter. I had no reason to kill either one. My God, man, you're talking about my daughter."

"Your wife was having an affair. She told you, right?"

"Yes, she was moving to a hotel that night and taking Emma. She was talking about leaving the city and going home to Texas. That's why I was with Hugh and not at home or the office. The thought of going home and not seeing Emma was just too hard."

"But she didn't go to a hotel, did she?"

"I guess she didn't, and I can't explain why."

"You're worth a lot of money, aren't you, sir?"

"Yes."

"And if your wife divorced you, she would get half of it and have a substantial stake in your company. Is that correct?"

"She could have had all my money. All I wanted was my daughter. Unlike some people, money doesn't mean anything to me."

"Says the man with lots of it," Flores said.

"Okay. We are done here," Roddy said. "If you want to talk to my client again be sure to go through me. Let's go, Russell."

As soon as the doors closed behind them, Roddy put his hand on Russell's arm. "That better be the last time you go off on a rant declaring your innocence without talking to me first. If you want me to represent you, shut up and let me do my job."

Russell looked surprised. He opened his mouth and then closed it and nodded.

∾

THE NOVEMBER SUN shone brightly in the clear blue sky, and the snow-covered Sandia Mountains glistened in the distance when the two men walked outside. Russell wasn't surprised to see Magdalena sitting on a bench under the skeleton branches of a large cottonwood tree that had shed its leaves for the winter.

She wore a Colorado University hooded sweatshirt, jeans, and boots. Her curly black hair bounced around her shoulders as she got up and made her way toward him. Russell caught his breath and thought he would never get tired of looking at this woman.

He enveloped her in his arms and held her for a long time without speaking, and then he finally said, "I told you not to come. I didn't know how long we'd be, but I'm happy to see you."

"What happened? What took so long?"

"Bentley turned the case over to the locals, and the lead detective's got a burr up his butt," Roddy said. "I think he's trying to punch holes in Russell's alibi. Let's go across the street to Starbucks, so we can talk."

After they got their drinks, Maggie tipped the vanilla latte to her mouth and then licked her lips. Russ hadn't taken his eyes off her. Maggie gripped his hand and squeezed. "I've got to tell you both something. I don't know what it means, but it scares me a little. After you and Hugh left last night, Bella said something to me." She looked searchingly into Russ's eyes and said, "Bella said Hugh was lying. About what, she doesn't know. She only knew that not everything he said was the whole truth."

"If he was lying about being with you, the police will find out. Hell, I'll find out," Roddy said looking at Russ.

"I remember Hugh meeting me at the office, which at the time I thought was odd, because he works in the warehouse and doesn't usually come to the corporate office building. But he was there, and he did ask me to come out for a drink. He said he'd talked to Sarah, and that he knew I might need a friend."

"Did you think that was strange?" Maggie said.

"Not at the time," Russell said, "but now..."

"Then what do you remember?" Maggie said.

"It was cold outside. I hadn't taken a jacket, and I remember being relieved when we got inside the bar. Then, I was drinking shots of something. Might have been tequila. I'm not a big drinker. Not even in college. After that, things get foggy. The next thing I remember was being at my house, and they were telling me there was a fire and Sarah and Emma were dead. The rest of the next few days were a blur."

"That means you don't remember drinking with Hugh all night? He said you got a message on your phone about the fire, and you two took a taxi to your house. Do you remember that?"

"No," Russ said and rubbed his fingers over his face and eyes. He hadn't gotten any sleep the last few nights and was beyond tired. "I don't know where my phone is. I think I lost it at the bar."

"Did you know about Hugh and Sarah?" Roddy asked.

"What? No, what about them?" Shock and anger lit up his eyes.

"He was sleeping with Sarah. Evidently, it had been going on for quite some time."

Russell seemed to deflate like a balloon and was glad he was sitting down. He had known his marriage was in trouble, and it had been a matter of time before it ended, but he hung on for Emma. The idea that Sarah and Hugh could have betrayed him was beyond comprehension.

175

She'd told him there was someone else, but in his wildest dreams, he wouldn't have guessed the man to be his brother Hugh.

"This changes everything, doesn't it?" he said stating the obvious.

"Yes, it most definitely could," Roddy said. "If Hugh's story is only partially true, and you weren't together the whole night, maybe it was to his advantage for the police to think so. Maybe Hugh was the one who needed an alibi."

"I can't believe Hugh could have done that. Not to Emma. He's a screwed-up guy, but he's not evil," Russell said.

"I guess we'll have to see, won't we?" Maggie said. "It will be interesting to find out what he's lying about."

CHAPTER 21

Russell and Maggie took a private car service to a sprawling two-story brown stucco building on the north side of town. Maggie stepped out of the car as her eyes roamed over the landscape.

"It's beautiful here in the desert with the mountains surrounding us," Maggie said. She looked down at her clothes and said, "I wasn't expecting to meet your colleagues today, or I would have worn something more appropriate than this old sweatshirt."

"You look amazing, and it wouldn't matter if you were wearing a burlap sack," Russell said.

"Have you been in contact with anyone here since you left, or did you walk off into the mountains without a word? That's something I could see you doing."

"I wasn't that rude. I made a quick call to Darren after I knew my trip was going to last longer than a few days, but it's been months since I've spoken to him again. He is perfectly capable of running things without me. He's more of the day-to-day operations guy, and I'm more the technical guy."

"You mean you're the guy with the ideas, and he handles the contracts and money."

"I didn't say that."

"You didn't have to," Maggie smiled and kissed him on the cheek. "It's so good to have you out of that horrible jail. I'm sorry they put you through all that hell."

"It's still not over," Russell said and gently ran his fingers down her face. "They could still arrest me."

"The police have their suspicions but no evidence. The truth will come out. Bella said as much. We will overcome all obstacles if we work together."

"Thank you for your belief in me. I don't think I would be able to get through all of this without you." His large hand covered hers. "Let's go see what's going on with my company. Hopefully, I still have one."

Maggie thought Bella would have described Darren Hess as "man pretty." He had delicate features and pale blue eyes. His brown hair with a slight graying at the temples was expertly cut. Maggie guessed he was close to six feet tall, but he seemed dwarfed by Russell's larger frame and height.

He rose when they walked into the office and smiled showing a row of dazzling white teeth. "Russ, where the hell have you been? Olive said someone called yesterday and said that you were in town."

"That someone was me," Maggie said.

"Darren, this is Magdalena Morales. I've been staying with her and her great-grandmother for the last several weeks."

Darren's gaze took in Maggie, and she noticed his eyes

lingered a little too long on her breasts. A noise in the hallway diverted Russell's attention, and she was sure Russell had not noticed Darren's lack of manners.

Maggie forced out the words, "It's nice to meet you, Darren," even though she didn't mean them. Maggie's many years of living with Bella had taught her to read a person's character. It usually took a while to see deep enough inside a person to make a fair judgment. Darren Hess was easy. Sadly, sizing up her ex-husband had not been so simple.

Maggie heard a squeal and saw a tall, blonde woman smother Russ in a warm embrace. "Oh, Russell, it is so good to have you back. Where have you been? We've all been worried something terrible had happened to you. Darren and I were talking about hiring a private investigator to find you."

Maggie watched Russell disentangle himself from the woman and turn toward her. "Olive, I would like you to meet Magdalena Morales."

"Oh, yes, I spoke to you on the phone. How nice of you to bring Russell back to us. I've been trying to get the software prototypes up and running, but without Russell's guidance, it's been difficult. I'm good," she said with a laugh, "but Russell is brilliant."

"Olive is the chief software engineer for the company and has been with us almost since the beginning. I'm sure she's exaggerating my abilities."

Olive Greeley was a sophisticated woman in her late thirties with a warm, welcoming smile. She was dressed impeccably in a charcoal gray suit showing off her toned body and exceptionally long legs. Maggie should have hated her on sight, but she didn't. The woman seemed to be genuine. It was evident that she thought very highly of Russell.

"Let's all sit down," Russell said. "I've got some things to talk about."

"Do you want coffee?" said Olive. "I can have them bring some in for us."

"Not me," Maggie said.

"Nor me. Magdalena and I stopped for coffee on the way."

"What's going on?" Olive said in a rush of words. "The police were here a few weeks ago. They were asking questions about you and Sarah. About your marriage and the success of the company."

"The medical examiner has ruled Sarah's and Emma's deaths as a homicide," Russell said. "I'm surprised it hasn't been on the news yet. I'm sure it will be sooner or later."

Olive gasped, and Darren turned white. "No, you can't mean that." She turned in her seat toward Darren. "When they spoke to you, did they say anything about their suspicions?"

"No, not a word," Darren said and looked at Russell. "The detective asked me how well I knew your wife and if you ever confided in me about your marriage. I told them that, as your business partner, I knew Sarah casually. Sometimes, if Sarah thought the company should be represented, I escorted her to business or charity functions that you didn't want to attend. But I didn't tell them anything about your marriage, Russell, because I didn't know anything."

Maggie noticed that Darren seemed uncomfortable. He rubbed his fingers together in a nervous gesture and tapped his foot.

"They asked me about what we did here at the company. I explained about our software designs." Darren looked down at his desk and then back up at Russell. "Come to think of it, there was one strange thing they asked."

"What was that?" Olive said.

"They asked if it was possible to start a fire from a distance. I laughed at first, and then I realized they were serious."

"What did you say?" Russell asked.

"I said theoretically it was possible. I explained that a smartphone could control any household appliance if the phone had the proper app installed and that it possibly could start a fire."

"Yes," said Olive. "They asked me the same thing. I said I certainly wasn't the expert, but we did develop software for smart homes as one of our products."

Maggie hesitated to get into the conversation, but the question needed to be asked. "What did you say about Russell's and Sarah's relationship?"

"I …" she looked at Russell and softly said, "I'm sorry Russell, I told them the things you told me. I couldn't lie."

What things? Maggie thought. What things had he told this woman that would lead the police to believe he killed his family?

"Please tell us what's going on," Darren said.

"The authorities have questioned me about the murders," Russell said. "Fortunately, I seem to have an alibi from Hugh, thus no arrest, but I remain a person of interest."

Olive stood up, anger rising in her eyes. "That is horrible. How dare they accuse you of killing your little girl.

No one that knows you, Russell, will ever believe that. Thank heavens for Hugh. Never much cared for the man, a little too sleazy for me." She looked at Russell. "Sorry, I know he's your brother and all, but I'm glad he can vouch for your whereabouts the night they died."

"They know Sarah was having an affair with him, and if Hugh can be believed, there was someone else besides him. I'm sure they will be looking at that person too."

If it were possible for Darren to get any paler, he would have become translucent. Damn, Maggie thought, that SOB was the other man who had been sleeping with Sarah.

∼

THEY TOOK an elevator to the lowest level of the building where the employees parked their vehicles. Maggie saw the lights blink on a dark blue Trailblazer and followed Russell to the passenger side. He opened the door for her, and as soon as he was seated behind the wheel, she opened her mouth to speak.

Before she could, Russ slammed his hand against the console and said, "Damn, was everyone in my company sleeping with my wife except for me?"

"You knew?"

"Not for sure. Not until today. Darren couldn't even look me in the eye. I've known him since we were in college and considered him a friend as well as a business partner. What is wrong with me that two men I trusted have betrayed me?"

Maggie didn't know what to say, and he obviously

wouldn't want her sympathy. They drove out of the lot in the direction of the hotel.

Russ glanced at her and said, "You suspected, didn't you?"

Maggie nodded and said, "It was pretty obvious. If it's any consolation, I think he feels bad about doing it, or maybe he feels bad because he knows he's going to get caught."

When they pulled up to a red light, Russ said, "Come here." He pulled her into his arms and held her tightly until a car honked behind them. As the SUV moved forward with the traffic, Russell said softly, "I don't know where to go from here, Magdalena. I just don't know."

CHAPTER 22

Russell stood in front of the bathroom mirror in the hotel suite while wiping off the last traces of shaving cream from his face. He had to go into work today but would much rather climb back into the warm bed and cover his head and cuddle next to a sleeping Magdalena.

They'd been up talking until late in the evening. Roddy took them out to dinner at one of the many Mexican restaurants in Old Town Albuquerque. He and Magdalena pushed the food around on their plates pretending to eat while Roddy and Bella seemed to have boisterous appetites. When Russell teased Bella about it, she'd replied that she was old and didn't plan on wasting any of her dinners. She didn't have that many left. Bella always had a way of elevating his mood.

When Roddy told everyone that he'd spoken with one of his friends at the Sheriff's Department in Angel Falls and that Lyman had been arrested and charged with embezzlement, Russell and Magdalena had done a dignified version of a high five. Bella being Bella had lifted her glass of wine and said, "Karma is a beautiful thing."

Roddy also said the state police were investigating the sheriff's behavior and his close ties to Lyman. Although no charges had been filed, he was temporarily relieved of his position, and a petition was circulating for a recall election.

Russell realized that yesterday had been an emotional day for both of them. It had its ups, but there were a lot more downs. For now, he was a free man, but the thought of another shoe dropping terrified him. What if revealing Hugh's duplicity would cause the police to train their full attention on him? How could he defend himself when he didn't know what happened?

Perhaps Roddy would find something when he interviewed the waitress from the bar. And perhaps the real killer would walk into the police department today and confess. *Yeah, and pigs can fly.*

∽

Maggie stretched, yawned, and looked at the empty place beside her in the bed. Russ was gone, and she hadn't heard a sound. She must have been dead to the world. Her dreams about the little girl had not been with her since the night she and Russ first made love. She had yet to voice out loud what she knew to be the truth. She was pregnant, and it had happened that first night because they hadn't taken any precautions. She knew she should tell Russ, but she wanted to wait until the right time.

Bella sat drinking room service coffee at the small table and eating what looked like the remnants of bacon and eggs. "You're certainly not watching your cholesterol lately," Maggie said.

"I like this kind of living. People are bringing me my food on a tray. Getting used to it for when you put me in the old folks' home."

"Uh huh, I can see that happening. You're ready to go home, aren't you?"

"Yes, I miss my mountains. The ones here are okay, but it's not Cielo Verde. I know we can't go yet. We need to see this through, mija. This isn't the end of it. Russell needs us."

Maggie heard the loud ring of the hotel room's phone on the desk. She answered and was surprised when she heard Olive Greely's greeting.

"Magdalena, this is Olive Greely. Russell said he didn't think you had made plans for the day. I've got a meeting later this morning, but I would love to take you and your great-grandmother to lunch."

"I'm meeting with someone later this afternoon, but lunch sounds like fun," Maggie said. "I'll check with Bella and see what her plans are."

"Fine, how about I pick you up in front of the hotel around eleven-thirty? Will that work for you?"

Maggie agreed, hung up the phone, and turned to Bella. "That was Olive Greely, Russ' co-worker and friend. She wants to take us to lunch. I wonder why?"

"Maybe she wants to check out the competition," Bella said putting the last piece of toast in her mouth.

"I don't think so. I didn't get that vibe. They seemed to be close, but I didn't detect any romantic overtones, especially on Russ's side."

"It will be interesting for you to find out. It might be

better if you go by yourself. I plan on visiting San Felipe Church and having a nice stroll around the plaza. I can gather my thoughts and maybe things will become clearer to me."

∼

AFTER A SCRUMPTIOUS LUNCH at a quaint little café that Olive said had the best bread in New Mexico, Maggie had yet to discover why the invitation had been offered. They'd chatted through the meal, but mostly they discussed Maggie's life, the lodge, and her first meeting with Russ. She and Olive concurred that Russell was a man of few words until you got to know him.

"I'd like to show you something," Olive said. "Do you have the time?"

Maggie looked at her watch and decided she still had a few hours to kill. "Sure, I guess so. Where are we going?"

Olive shifted the brown BMW convertible into third gear, and Maggie noticed they were driving toward the Sandia's. Olive hadn't answered her question, but three minutes later they stopped in front of a home that fire had partially destroyed. It was a large, two-story hidden in the shadows of the mountain. Once it had been magnificent, but now it only looked sad and neglected.

"This was Russell's home. Where Sarah and Emma died."

Spacing the words out evenly, Maggie said, "Why did you bring me here?"

"I want you to understand what a number that woman did on him. I noticed you took an interest when I told

Russ I had to tell the police some of the things he said to me."

"Yes, but if Russ wants me to know, he'll tell me."

"Russ and I come from similar backgrounds. You do know about his background, don't you?"

"Yes, he's spoken to me about his childhood."

"I promised myself I would never be poor again, and once I left home, I've been able to keep that promise. Russ didn't have the same needs as I did. He wanted to be successful, but his definition of success didn't include becoming wealthy. This house was Sarah's idea, but as the company started to take off and money was no object, she wanted more."

Maggie felt uncomfortable talking to Olive about Sarah's shortcomings, but she couldn't stop herself from listening.

"Russ keeps everything very close to the vest, you know, but on occasion, he would confide his frustration with Sarah's values. He wanted Emma to grow up with everything she needed, but not necessarily everything she wanted. I never understood what Russell saw in Sarah. She was beautiful; I'll give you that, but she was also spoiled, vain, and shallow. Then, after they were married, and Emma was born so soon, I counted up the months. That's when I knew why."

"He married Sarah because she was pregnant?"

"Russ is nothing if not an honorable man. He loved that little girl more than anyone. He would have been devastated to find out she wasn't his."

"What? No, that can't be true."

"You don't think so?"

"No, I ..." she touched her stomach lightly and said, "No, I know Emma was Russell's child," Maggie said.

"Well, there were rumors," Olive said, "but I guess it doesn't really matter now, does it? Russell seems to be happy, or at least as happy as he can be under the circumstances. I think you must be good for him. He doesn't make friends easily. For his sake, I'm sorry that he found out about Darren."

"You knew about the affair?"

"Oh, yes, Darren confessed to me after the first time they were together. I think he tried to stay away, but lust can be a powerful thing."

"You and Russell?" Maggie said holding her breath.

"Oh no, never. Only friendship. Russell took vows, and he would never break them. But Darren and I have been off and on for years. Currently, we are on. Do you and Russell have plans?"

"No, no plans. Bella and I are here for support. Hopefully, everything will be settled soon, and after Russ is fully exonerated, I'll go back home."

"You and your great-grandmother have been such a blessing to him. You took him in when he was at the lowest point of his life. As one of his oldest friends, I wanted to thank you. Hopefully, you and I can become friends too."

CHAPTER 23

After learning that Russell and Hugh had gone to The Thirsty Lizard in Albuquerque on the night of the fire at Russell's home, Roddy made it a point to visit there and get as much information as he could.

The bartender didn't know a waitress named Tara or Scarlett, and he had not been working on the night in question. He had only been on the job for six months.

"Is there anyone on the staff who has been here for a year or so? How about the manager?" Roddy said.

"The owner manages the business himself. This place gets pretty crowded after people get off work, so he's always here after five 0'clock."

Roddy looked at his phone. It was almost five, so he planned to hang around. "You have anything to eat that you'd recommend?"

"Oh, yeah. You need to try the chile relleno nachos. They're to die for."

"Sounds good. I'll take some, and a Sprite if you have one."

"Coming up," the man said and made his way to the computer to type in the order.

When he came back with the Sprite, Roddy said, "You have CCTV in here?"

"Not inside. We record the parking lot. That's where all the fights happen. Sometimes people get pissed off and end up breaking out somebody else's car windows, especially on the expensive cars."

"Geez," said Roddy. "Should I be worried?"

"Depends," he said. "What are you driving?"

Roddy took a sip of the Sprite, swallowed, and said. "I'm in a Ford."

The bartender scratched his beard. "A Mustang?"

Roddy smiled. "Nope, it's a pickup."

The bartender grinned. "Relax. Your food will be up soon."

~

THE OWNER WALKED in about fifteen minutes to five. He hung his jacket on a hook behind the bar and tied on an apron. His eyes surveyed the room as he wiped down the already clean bar. He greeted regulars and worked his way toward Roddy.

"Good evening," he said. "Thanks for coming in. Can I get you a refill on anything?"

"No thanks," Roddy held out his hand. "I'm waiting to talk to you. My name is Roddy Eastman, and I'm an attorney here in Albuquerque."

"Sam Fedderson. Nice to meet you." The other man's handshake was friendly, but the look in his eyes was not. "Okay? Let's get to it. What do you want to know?"

"My client's name is Russell Zarek, and he and his stepbrother, Hugh Powell, came in here to have a few drinks on the 2nd of May."

"So did a lot of guys."

Roddy pulled two photos from his shirt pocket and held them out. "I don't suppose you would remember them?"

He flashed a look at the photos. "Sorry, no."

"Is there a chance we could see them coming or going on the parking lot videos?"

"When did you say they were here?"

"May 2nd."

"Then, no. There's no chance. We wouldn't save those unless there was an incident. In that case, we call the cops and turn the video over to them. We haven't had a problem here in ages. In fact, the last one was in October when the Red Sox beat the Dodgers."

"I see. Here's another thing. Did you have a waitress working here on that particular night who has since moved on?"

"Those girls don't stay long. Not the biggest tippers in here," he said. "I can look it up in my records if you give me a few minutes," he said. "I have to wait until Tim gets back from his break."

"Sure. Thanks," Roddy said.

Thirty minutes later he was back with a name. "Found her. She was only here for about six weeks or so and then moved on to Santa Fe. She knew somebody who opened up a new restaurant. Minimum wage up there is the highest in the state. Tips are great, I hear."

"Any chance she told you the name of the place?" Roddy said.

"Yeah. I wrote her a recommendation." He tapped a folded slip of paper and handed it to Roddy. "She's a good waitress. Her name is Melanie," he said.

Roddy grinned. "Last name Wilkes, I presume?"

"Pardon me?" Sam looked confused. "No, her last name is Wolf."

"Never mind. Thanks for the information. I appreciate it."

IN WINTER, the drive to Santa Fe would take a little over an hour as long as Interstate 25 was plowed and free of ice. The highway was clear today, and it was one of those sunny, turquoise-sky days in New Mexico. The high altitude and wide-open spaces eliminated pollution, and puffy clouds dotted the sky like dumplings.

Roddy had a fleeting thought that such a day would be wasted since he would be indoors much of the time, but this trip might be important. He'd rather be hauling hay or working with his horses, but if he could find this waitress, she could be the key to keeping his client out of jail.

He pulled up in front of a pink stucco building with a door painted turquoise. It was between the lunch and the dinner crowd, but close to the magic, happy hour time, so he hoped someone would be available to help him.

He waited at the hostess stand until a thirtyish looking woman saw him and quickly moved to acknowledge him. "Oh, I'm sorry. I didn't see you standing there. Would you like a table or a booth?"

"Either would be fine, but I may not be staying for dinner. I am looking for someone who works here. I am an attorney from Albuquerque, and I need to ask her a few questions."

She took a step to the side of the tall, wooden stand and he could see that she was younger than he first thought. It was her clothes that had made her look older than her years. She wore the requisite black dress with a white, ruffled apron, black leggings, and flat leather shoes. He assumed the restaurant wanted its employees to look respectable and feel comfortable. "Is somebody in trouble?"

"Oh, no. Not at all. I am trying to get some information from a waitress that waited on my client. This woman could be a big help to me."

"What is her name? Maybe I can help."

"Her name is Melanie Wolf. She used to work at The Thirsty Lizard in Albuquerque."

She leaned against the wooden stand as if to steady herself, and then held out her hand. "I guess this is your lucky day," she said.

~

AFTER CLEARING it with her boss, she led him to a booth in the back of the restaurant, placed two glasses of ice water on the table, and slid onto the leather bench across from Roddy.

"I'm Roddy Eastman," he said and smiled. "May I call you Melanie?" he asked.

"Sure. That's fine." She picked up the crisp, white napkin and twisted it in her fingers.

"I have a client who says he had a few beers with his

brother in The Thirsty Lizard on May 2nd. If that's true, it could help his case." He pulled the two photos out of his shirt pocket and placed them face up on the table.

She put one finger out and moved the photos closer to her and studied them for a moment. "Oh, sure. I knew this guy. He came into the bar a lot after work and had a few beers."

"Was he generous with his tips?" he said.

"Not so much. He was a little flirty. His name is Hugh."

"How about the other guy?"

"I remember him because he left a big tip."

"Do you remember his name?"

"I think so. This one, the big guy, is Rusty or Russell or something like that. Right?"

Roddy nodded. "Yes, his name is Russell."

"And this guy" she pointed to Hugh's photo, "was a frequent flyer. They should put his name on that stool."

"You do remember; that's great. We know by their credit card receipts that they were at the bar on May 2nd. Do you remember that night?"

"I think so. We were slammed because Albuquerque had a bar crawl that night."

"Hugh says they were both drinking heavily and both of them got pretty wasted."

An arched eyebrow indicated her surprise. "I don't think that's the way it happened."

Roddy waited for her to continue. He took a drink of water and set the glass back down on the table.

"Hugh kept ordering pitchers of beer with tequila chasers, but he would pour a glass and hand it to Russell. The big guy is the one who was chugging them down."

"And what time was it when they left?"

"I'm not exactly sure, but I guess it was around midnight give or take a few minutes."

"Did you suggest that they call a cab or an Uber?"

"Nope. No need for that. Hugh seemed pretty sober when they left."

CHAPTER 24

Hugh Powell was having a bad day. Now that his brother knew about his affair with Sarah, he felt like the scum of the earth. He had always thought of Russell as the guy with all the money and all the luck, but Russell's marriage had been a disaster, and he took no pleasure in how the truth about Russell's cold, unfaithful wife was being thrown in his brother's face.

Since Hugh's involvement with Sarah had become common knowledge, he knew he was in trouble. Big trouble. The secrets he'd been keeping for over a year were all coming to light.

He made his way across the room to pick up the ringing phone lying on the bedside table. "This is Hugh," he said and listened for a few moments. When he ended the call, he knew his day had gone from bad to worse.

WHAT WAS it about the odor in the police station that made him want to run out the door? The sweat? The commingling of body odors? The stale coffee in stained mugs? Hugh wasn't sure, but he had to force his face to relax the furrow between his eyes and command his feet to move one in front of the other.

"Hugh Powell," he said at the front desk to the officer wearing a navy-blue shirt that was stretched over his protruding belly.

The officer looked up from the papers on a clipboard and crooked an eyebrow as if to say, "And …?"

"I'm here to speak to Detective Flores."

"Sure thing. Follow that hallway to the end. When you get inside the room, he's at the second desk on the left."

Hugh did as he was told. He was surprised to see only nine desks in the room. Tables arranged along the wall held fax machines, a laser printer, and copy machines. Four of the desk chairs were occupied. The chair in front of desk number two was empty. "Excuse me," he said. "Anybody seen Detective Flores?"

"I'm here," Flores said as he made his way into the room with a white banker's box in his hands. He plopped it down on the desk and reached out to shake hands. "Good to see you, Mr. Powell. Please have a seat."

Hugh sat down on an uncomfortable folding chair. He knew why the police department could not afford better furniture. There had been problems with funding in Albuquerque for years. The crime rate in the city necessitated spending every available dollar on getting more officers trained and on the streets. Comfortable chairs were not a top priority.

"I'm not sure why I'm here, Detective. I've been over my statement twice at least."

"Yes, that's true, but perhaps some of the things you said in your statement weren't accurate."

"Yeah? Like what?"

"Well," Flores said, "for instance, you never told us that you were having an affair with your brother's wife."

Hugh shuffled his feet. "You never asked me."

Flores smiled. "Can I get you some coffee or water, Mr. Powell?"

"No, thanks. Anyway, that information wasn't relevant."

"Everything is relevant in a homicide case. The more information we have, the better."

"Tell me about your affair with Mrs. Zarek."

"First, I wouldn't call it an affair. I snuck up the stairs a few times, and we got it on. Nothing romantic, I can assure you. Sarah had plenty of lovers, not only me. It's a wonder I didn't bump into some other schmuck on my way out."

"Is that how you see yourself? As a schmuck?"

Hugh's eyes narrowed. "Not usually. I do all right. She's the one who had self-esteem issues."

"Can you tell me what you mean by that?"

"Sarah slept with almost anybody who could get his zipper down. I didn't know that at first, but when I figured it out, I kept my distance."

"Did you ever consider telling your brother what you knew about his wife?"

"What? And hurt his feelings like that?" he looked shocked.

"Yes, but you were sleeping with her, too," his voice held a challenge.

"I wasn't doing it to hurt him. She was hard to resist, but I would never have told him."

"Let me run this by you," the detective said. "Suppose Russell did know about your sexual encounters with his wife. Would that make him mad enough to kill her, you think?"

Hugh's laugh had a sharp edge. "Russell is not like that. He's no killer. Besides, I told you that he was with me that night."

"You did, yes, and he said the same thing. But your account of that night and the one Russell gave are different. Why do you suppose that is?"

"How should I know?" he said. He swallowed and took a deep breath. "What did he say?"

"He said he doesn't remember what happened that night after he left The Thirsty Lizard. He remembers getting in his car but doesn't remember driving it."

Hugh didn't say anything.

"Your brother's biggest regret is not answering the warning text that came in on his phone. He thinks his ex-wife and his little girl might still be alive if he had rushed to the house."

Still no response from Hugh.

"I'm talking about the text that came in on the smart home application notifying him that there was a fire at his home."

The look of anguish on Hugh's face was impossible to hide. "Well, he's wrong."

"What do you mean?"

"Russ never saw that message. I saw the text come in

and read it. He was out cold. I couldn't wake him. I took his phone, left him in his car, jumped in mine and drove like a bat out of hell. By the time I got to the house, the fire department had cordoned off the perimeter, and I couldn't do a damn thing but watch them bring out the bodies." He put his head in his hands and sat there slumped in the chair.

Detective Flores stood, walked around in front of Hugh's chair, and leaned casually against the wall. "Mr. Powell, what kind of car do you drive?"

"What?" Hugh asked with deceptive calm. "Why is that relevant?"

"Please answer the question."

"It's nothing to brag about. A used Jeep, okay?"

"What model and year?"

"It's a 2015 Cherokee."

"Four-wheel drive?"

"Yes, why?"

"Just asking. What color is it?"

"What's going on here? Why all this interest in my car?"

"Color?" the detective repeated.

Hugh's lips thinned with anger. "It's white."

The detective pushed away from the wall and moved back to his desk chair. He put his arms on the desk and leaned forward towards Hugh.

"I'm glad you were smart enough to describe your car truthfully because I already looked it up with the Motor Vehicle Division."

"You what?" His voice registered alarm. "And you did that because?"

"Because one of Sarah's neighbors saw your car in the

driveway of Sarah Zarek's house on the night of the fire. His dog woke him up about twelve-forty, and he took it outside."

"How do you know it was my car?"

The detective locked eyes with Hugh and held his gaze. "Was it? You tell me."

Hugh tried to swallow his panic. He looked around the room as if searching for an escape route.

"Would you like some water?" Mr. Powell.

"Yes," he said while hoping for a few moments to think.

The detective opened a mini-fridge behind his desk and handed him a bottle of Dasani.

After he took a long drink, he took a few deep breaths to steady his voice and then said, "Yes. It was my car."

"What were you doing there that night?"

"I went to tell Sarah that we should disclose our relationship to Russell before he found out some other way. I kept his phone because I was afraid she was going to tell him before I could."

"What did she say?"

She looked down her skinny nose at me and said, "What relationship?'"

"And how did that make you feel?" the detective asked.

"Like I'd been punched in the gut. I knew we weren't in love with each other, but I thought I was more to her than just a good lay."

"Did the two of you argue?"

He suddenly felt a wave of bitterness. "She wasn't worth fighting for. She was a tease and a money-grubbing bitch."

"Is that why you killed her?"

Hugh's body stiffened in shock. "I did not! I did not kill anybody, and you can't prove that I did." Before the detective could stop him, Hugh rushed out of the room leaving the door wide open behind him.

CHAPTER 25

"Dare I ask about your day?" Olive asked Darren as she slipped out of her cherry red skirt.

She'd worn her power suit today to meet with Russell's new girlfriend. She was surprised to find Magdalena sweet and honest—a far cry from Sarah.

"Well, I certainly didn't have a good day. Did you expect me to?" Darren said.

"I guess not, but then Sarah wasn't exactly my type." She walked over to Darren and gave him a long, lingering kiss.

"What am I going to do? This is all such a mess."

"You honestly believed that Russell would never find out about you and his wife? Sweetheart, you can't be that naïve."

"How did he find out? Did you tell him?"

Olive laughed and started to unbuckle his belt. "What would be my purpose for doing that? I'm fond of the man. I wouldn't want to hurt him. If I was going to tell him, I sure would have done it before the little bitch died, but from what I understand she told him. Was she leaving him for you?"

"Who told you that?" He pushed her away and discarded his shirt and tie.

"Did she tell you she aborted the baby?"

His face registered a shock of genuine surprise.

"You didn't know? I assumed she had told you. After all, that is the way she got Russell to marry her. Was the baby yours?"

When he didn't reply, she moved closer to him and kissed him again. "Well, was it?" Her tone held a challenge.

"I don't know. She said it was, but then I wasn't the only man she was sleeping with. It could have been Russell's. I didn't know she got rid of it."

"It wasn't his."

"Sarah told you that?"

"No, Russell did. Oh, don't look so shocked. He didn't know about the baby or the abortion. He would have kicked her to the curb if he had." She rubbed her hands down his flat sculptured abs and kissed his nipples. "Russell confided in me that things were not going well, and they were sleeping in separate rooms. We're friends. We've all known each other for a long time. Friends help friends, especially friends with benefits."

"I don't know what he's going to do. You have to help me. Without Russell ... well without him, there is no company. I can't come up with the programs, and you've proven these last few months that you're no Russell," Darren said.

Olive stopped and stepped away from Darren; her eyes darkened with anger. She picked up his shirt and tie and threw them at him. "I think it's time for you to go. I didn't ask you here to insult me. I was going to try and smooth things over between the two of you, but now I think I'll let you sink on your own."

Darren put his head in his hands. "I didn't want things to turn out like this. I never wanted Russell to find out."

Olive took pity on him and sat down beside him, touching him lightly on his arm. "What did he say to you?"

"When he asked if I was having an affair with Sarah, I vehemently denied it. I said there was nothing between us, and if she had told him so, it was a lie. I said I was his friend and wouldn't do that to him." Darren shuddered and closed his eyes. "She was so damn beautiful, Olive. Russell didn't make her happy, and I thought I did. Right up to the end, I thought I did."

"My God, Darren," Olive exclaimed, "did you kill her?"

Darren got up and opened the door. "If I did, you'd be the last person I would tell."

∽

"Mr. Hess, there is a Detective Flores here to speak with you," a female voice said in a pronounced Spanish accent over his intercom.

Darren swallowed, and his heart raced. "Detective Flores, all right, give me a minute to finish up. I'll be out in a minute."

His stomach clenched, and he began to sweat. He took a calming breath and opened his office door. "Good morning, Detective, nice to see you again. Please come in. Claudia, please get the detective a coffee."

"Thank you, ma'am. If I could have cream and a couple of sugars, that would be great."

Darren watched Flores' eyes take in the office and furnishings and then sit in the chair closest to the desk. "I don't see any family pictures. I take it you're not married?"

There were several framed photographs of Darren alone. In one, he was dressed in snow gear with goggles pushed up over his cap and a pensive look on his face. He was standing behind a snowboard. In another, he was standing on a sandy beach while holding a surfboard under his arm and smiling at someone in the distance. Hung on the far wall were various certificates and plaques and a large, professionally framed diploma from The Massachusetts Institute of Technology.

"No, not unless you count being married to my job."

"I see you're into board sports."

"Yes, are you?"

"In my teens, I was pretty mean competition at the skate park, but I've never tried the snow, and I've never been near an ocean. I'm a homeboy."

Darren didn't know how to respond, so he sat as patiently as he could and was relieved when Claudia brought the coffee and gave him a soft smile as she said, "Can I bring you anything else?"

"No, we're good. Please hold my calls." Darren looked at the man sitting in front of him. The detective wore a blue, long sleeve shirt, gray slacks, and a rumpled suit coat. He didn't look threatening, but Darren had seen enough TV crime shows to be concerned. A second visit from the police, and especially an unexpected visit, could not be a good thing.

"You don't look surprised to see me," Flores said.

"I don't know why you say that. Of course, I am. I don't know what else I can tell you that I didn't already say when we met several months ago."

"I have a few follow-up questions. You know, to tie up some loose ends." He took out a small notebook and a pen from his suit coat. "Let's see. Previously, you mentioned smart homes and how they work. Do you remember that?"

"Yes, of course. What about them?"

"You neglected to mention that you had one."

"Why would that have been relevant? Many of the employees in the company do. It's the up-and-coming thing."

"Hmm. All right. Perhaps I could get a list of those employees."

Darren laughed and said, "Why would I have a list? I'm the owner of the company. I don't know who has what; however, I've heard several people discuss it in passing."

"Oh, I see. How well did you know Mrs. Zarek?"

"As I told you before, I sometimes escorted her to functions. We were friends. Olive and I often had dinner with Russell and Sarah."

"Did you ever visit Mrs. Zarek when her husband was not at home?"

Darren looked nervously around the room and chose his words carefully. "Yes. That would have been one of those times when I needed to pick her up for a business dinner or reception."

"And this was with Mr. Zarek's approval?"

"It was at his request. What are you implying? Sarah and I were only friends."

"Did you see her on the day that she died?"

"I don't believe so. Let me look on my calendar." Darren opened the Google calendar and clicked on May. "No, I have nothing here. I was in the office all day, I believe."

"Hmm, that's very interesting. Your neighbor," Flores consulted his notebook and looked back at Darren, "a Mr. Stevens, remembers seeing an attractive blonde woman enter your house with you that day."

"I date lots of women. I'm sure it was another day, or the woman could have been Olive. She's often there."

Flores closed his notebook and said, "Okay, I guess that's all the questions I have at this time." He stood and started toward the door and, in his best Columbo move, turned around and said, "Oh, just one more thing. Mr. Stevens is quite sure it was that day because he knew you worked at Zarek International, and he remembers hearing about the fire and deaths the next morning. Isn't that interesting? I'll be in touch, Mr. Hess."

CHAPTER 26

Russell held a steaming cup of coffee while making his way from the break room back to his office. When he saw Detective Flores walking across the lobby toward the main doors, he stopped suddenly, and the hot liquid sloshed on his hand. "Damn," Russell said, shaking the scalding coffee from his hand. The curse had been loud enough to draw the other man's attention.

"Detective Flores, I didn't realize we had an appointment today. I've got a busy morning. If it won't take long, I can see you now, but if not, you'll need to reschedule." Starting for his office, Russell turned and said, "Oh, yeah, I almost forgot. I'm not supposed to speak to you without my attorney. He gets huffy when I do that." He was extremely pleased with the rebuff he had given the detective as he continued toward his office.

"No problem," Flores said walking swiftly to catch up. "I'm not here to see you today. I was having a conversation with your partner, Mr. Hess. If I promise not to ask any questions about you, can we talk for a minute?"

"You? Make a promise? Why do I not believe you? Come on in. I'll listen and I may or may not answer."

An oversized desk with three monitors, a laptop computer, and an additional keyboard comprised Russell's office. Behind the desk against the wall stood a tall bookcase with robotic children's toys and a framed photo of him with Emma sitting in his lap. The blinds were open on a large window facing the snow-covered mountain.

Russell removed the stack of papers on the chair so that the detective could be seated. "Sorry for the mess, but I usually don't have visitors. Darren takes care of most of the day-to-day stuff, which allows me to be left alone to work."

"I understand you graduated from MIT. I don't see your diploma hanging on the wall."

"Why would I want to do that? And, I thought you weren't asking questions about me."

"Sorry, I guess that was more of an observation than a question."

"And what does that tell you about me?"

"If I were a shrink, which I'm not, I would say you're not someone that needs or wants to draw attention to himself, and you're pretty self-confident."

"Okay, so why does that matter, and why do you care?"

"You make it very difficult not to like you, Mr. Zarek."

"Thank you, I guess, and call me Russell. I feel like we're old friends," he said with a slow, sarcastic smile.

"How long have you known Mr. Hess?"

"Since college. We went to school together. He was in management, and I studied computer technology. He was the frat boy, and I wasn't. I spent most of my time in the library or the computer lab. He needed some help on an assignment, and one of my professors asked me to see what I could do. We discovered we were from the same part of the world. Me from Tucumcari and Darren from right here in Albuquerque."

Flores took out his pen and notebook and said, "Mind if I write this down?"

"I'm not sure. I've got to be honest; you scare the shit out of me. Maybe I should call Roddy after all."

"Look, Russell, you and I want the same thing. We want to see whoever is responsible for your family's death brought to justice. I'm not trying to railroad you or anyone else. I am only looking for the truth. If you are telling the truth, and I'm inclined to believe that you are, then you have nothing to worry about from me."

"Fair enough." Russell leaned back in his chair. "Darren and I weren't great friends in school, but we were both ambitious and hungry. I knew crap about starting a business, but I had ideas for products. We put our heads together after graduation and started this company."

"And has your friendship grown over the years?"

"We socialized a little but not a great deal. He's a player. I never was."

"A player? You mean with women?"

"Yes, there have been several, but I don't believe he's ever been serious. He and Olive have been playing house off and on for years."

"And your wife?"

"What about her?"

"Don't play dumb, Russell. I thought we had gotten past that. Was he sleeping with your wife?"

"He says no. I confronted him earlier this week, and he denied it. He said if she told me that, she was lying."

"And do you believe him?"

"I want to. I have no proof that he was."

"What if I told you he was seen at his home with a beautiful blonde woman the day your wife died?"

∼

RUSSELL SAT at his desk staring at his computer while repeatedly doing the same thing and coming up with the same problem. *Wasn't that what Einstein said the definition of insanity was?* He couldn't block the image of Sarah and Darren together. Could he have been blind enough not to see it, and then stupid enough to believe Darren when he denied it?

He looked up as Olive breezed into the room with her usual, graceful elegance. He thought she was a gorgeous woman, but he'd never felt that zing with her. Today, she wore a form-fitting, light purple dress, and matching shoes. The woman had great legs.

They'd met right after Russell moved to Albuquerque. During the first year, when he and Darren had started the business, they worked out of a storefront in a run-down strip center on the south side of town. They'd introduced some products, and the company was on the verge of taking off. Russell happened to meet Olive at a conference and scooped her up after he read her impressive resume.

She was divorced, had no children, and wanted to relocate from California. Although she was a few years older than the two men who were fresh out of school, she seemed to fit in seamlessly. One night, after celebrating a successful launching of a new product, a drunken Olive had kissed Russell. If he'd given her any encouragement, they would have ended up in bed together, but he was glad now that they never did. Olive had never made another move on him, and they'd gone on to have a lasting friendship.

Olive tried to warn him about Sarah, and by the time he'd seen through Sarah's flawless face and model figure to the empty shell she was, she'd been pregnant with Emma, and he had proposed.

"Hey fella, what's going on?" Olive said. "I saw the law here earlier. Please tell me they don't still have you at the top of their list. Hugh gave you an alibi," she said and sat down gracefully and crossed her legs.

"Surprisingly, he didn't want to talk about me. He was interested in Darren."

"Darren? Surely not. He's a lot of things, but he's not a killer."

"Are you sure, or are you saying that because you're lovers?"

"Oh, come on, Russ. This is Dandy Dick Darren we're talking about. He's had lots of women; that's who he is. When we first got together way back when, I knew that we would never be exclusive. He isn't made that way. His relationship with Sarah would have been the same way."

"You're saying it's true, aren't you? He's the one she had the affair with, isn't he? She was leaving me for Darren and taking my daughter. It wasn't you going into Darren's house on the day she'd died, was it?"

"Why, did he say it was me?"

"No, it was something the detective mentioned."

"Look, Russ, it's over now. It's in the past. Sarah was a

disturbed little girl looking for love in all the wrong places. I don't know why she did what she did, and it's tragic that one of her lovers probably killed her, but it wasn't Darren. He wouldn't have the balls to pull off something like that."

"How long have you known what was going on? And don't you dare lie to me," Russell said.

"Not long, I promise. I spoke with Sarah briefly and knew she wasn't happy. She wanted more excitement. You know, to go out more and do more things." Olive moved closer to Russ and touched him tenderly on his shoulder. "She was young, Russ. She would have matured eventually." She squeezed his arm and moved away slightly.

His eyes studied her intently, but he did not say anything.

"Remember our conversation when you told me you were sleeping in separate bedrooms?" she continued. "I suspected she and Darren had become more than mere acquaintances, and it wasn't but a few days before Sarah died that I knew for sure."

She sat back down, and her expression was sad. "I was going to tell you, but then she died, and I thought there was no point. It would only hurt you, and now I'm so sorry that I didn't."

As she got up to leave, she said, "You know Darren would never have chosen Sarah over you. She was a pretty little thing, but she wasn't the Golden Goose to Darren like you are. Without you, this company would be nothing, and he knows it. He wouldn't throw it all away for a piece of … well, you know what I mean."

Darren closed his laptop and was in the process of putting it into the case to take home when he heard a knock on his door. "Who is it?" he said frustration evident in his reply.

"It's the Golden Goose," Russ said, pushing the door open.

Darren stood up and stumbled back against the wall as an angry, but controlled Russell approached him.

"R ... Russ," Darren managed to stammer. "What are you talking about?"

Russell didn't like to use his size to intimidate, but this time it gave him great delight to see the fear in the other man's eyes. "I think it would be a good idea for you to look for another office. This one has become too small for the both of us. Maybe something downtown?"

"What the hell is wrong with you, Russ? Are you crazy?"

"No, Darren. I've been kicking myself all afternoon while trying to understand why I failed to see what was right in front of my face. I am the world's biggest idiot. No more. This is it. I'm done. I don't want to see your face again unless it is absolutely necessary."

"Russ, what is it? What has someone told you? Whatever it is, I promise it's not true."

Russell raised his fist, and Darren flinched in expectation of a blow. "You are not worth it. You slept with my wife, and you may have killed my daughter. Get out of my sight," he said as his hand fell to his side, and he walked out the door.

CHAPTER 27

Roddy's phone rang before he had brewed his first cup of coffee. Crap, he thought, so much for an excellent start to my day. Then, he looked at the screen and saw Magdalena's name and smiled. "Maggie? Everything all right?"

"Well, everything except that the police suspect the man I love of being a murderer and Cielo Verde is not financially stable yet. Otherwise, yes, everything is fine."

He didn't know whether to laugh or to offer sympathy. Knowing Maggie, neither sentiment would be particularly appreciated. Instead, he tried to remain stoic yet supportive. It was a role he was used to playing with his clients. It was the *I'm here for you attitude* he wanted to project. Concerning Magdalena and Bella, that would always be exactly how he felt.

"So, you called me to tell me how fine you are? I already knew that, honey."

She didn't laugh. "No, Roddy. I hate to say this, but I called you for another favor."

"Speak to me," he said.

"Bella is getting restless. She misses Cielo Verde and has never liked being in the city. I can't take her home because I don't want to leave Russell alone right now."

"And you want me to do it, right?"

"Is that an impossible request? Say so if it is, and I'll figure out some other way."

"Not at all. I spend most weekends in Angel Falls with my parents. I have room for one small lady in my pickup. Can she be ready to go in the morning at about nine o'clock?"

"Oh, thank you, Roddy. I know she's going to be happy to go home. I owe you big time for everything you're doing for Russell and me."

~

BELLA TOOK a child's delight in the scenery on the winding road to Angel Falls. Nothing made her happier than being in the forest. She loved the smell of the pine trees, the sight of the blue sky above, and the occasional lucky sighting of wildlife like deer, turkeys, and once in a while a black bear. That city was for people who like the smell of car exhaust and the sounds of trucks, sirens, and fast-moving cars.

Roddy stopped the pickup in front of the lodge and helped Bella up the steps and into the living room. Expecting her return today, Billy and Dora had tidied up the house and started a blazing log fire. The tantalizing aroma of something spicy wafted from the kitchen.

"Hello, the house," Bella said and began shedding her scarf and hat. Boney rose from in front of the fireplace and made his way across the room. He still had a limp, but his tail wagged like a flag in the wind. Bella leaned down and hugged him and scratched him behind his ears.

"Oh, Mrs. Morales," Dora said as she came hurrying out of the kitchen. "So glad you're home. We've been keeping the lights on for you."

"Well, I should hope not," Bella said. "We have enough bills to pay without making our power bill even higher."

Dora's laughter bubbled. "Oh, no. That was a figure of speech," she said. "We opened up the house early this morning to get it ready for your return."

Bella ignored her explanation and took her place in her favorite chair. "Do you have any strong coffee ready? The brown water that came out of that machine in the hotel room tasted like burned paper."

Roddy deposited the luggage in Bella's room and turned to go. "Bella, I'll be at my parents' house or the store. If you need anything, you know you can call me. My phone number …"

"I know the number, Roddy Eastman. I've been doing business with your parents for decades. Now you go on. I need my peace and quiet."

He opened the door to leave, but before he closed it behind him, he heard Bella say, "And thank you, young man. You are a treasure."

⁓

THE NEXT MORNING when Bella woke up, she had a feeling that made it hard for her to breathe. Something was wrong. She knew it. The only thing that was going to make her feel better would be to read the cards. At least that way she would have some idea of where this ominous feeling was coming from.

She sat at her kitchen table and spread her cards the way she liked them. She took a quick read of the past and then turned over the cards to show the present. Yes, her previous interpretations had been correct, and the playful teasing she'd done with Maggie would turn out to be a reality. The Empress was a sure sign of pregnancy.

But this was a happy thing. Why the dreaded feeling? She looked to the cards for the future and shook her head when she saw secrets, pain, and loss.

Knowing this gave her no comfort; in fact, it piqued her curiosity. And when Bella Morales wanted information, nothing could stop her from finding out.

Nothing good ever came from keeping secrets, and Maggie was keeping a big one from Russell. Bella wanted to know why.

∽

RUSSELL STRUGGLED with the questions the police kept throwing at him. When he answered them, it brought back memories of Emma, and he found he had not even begun to heal from his loss. Now, the new homicide investigation was tearing off the scabs that were only beginning to form over his wounded heart. The only time he felt good was when he spent time with Maggie.

It had been so long since he had felt the peace and joy of being in love. Things had never been right with Sarah. He knew that now more than ever. Love wasn't about fighting and making up or slinging harsh words at one another and then whispering apologies and regrets. And, most of all, love wasn't about wild, aerobic sex.

His time with Maggie was slow and sweet and full of so much love he thought his heart would burst from his chest. She was a high-spirited woman, but not high-maintenance. She asked nothing of him, and he wanted to give her everything.

Their time together had been so short before trouble came to find him. He hoped they could steal a few hours or days to spend together before he was arrested. If he was arrested. If they could make a case against him. He had read about other innocent men who had gone to prison because the police could not find the real killer, so the husband had to be it. It was always the husband.

At least he had an alibi. His one ace in the hole. He and Hugh had never been close buddies, but his brother had come through for him this time, and he was grateful even though he could never forgive Hugh for betraying his trust and sleeping with Sarah. To this day, he had no memory of walking out of The Thirsty Lizard the night of the fire. When he woke up in his car, he couldn't find his phone. He still had no idea where it was. He thought he would ask Maggie to go with him to an electronics store so he could buy a new one. He was back in the real world again, so he should start acting like it.

His thoughts about Maggie made him wonder where she had gone. When he awoke, her side of the bed was empty, and her purse and shawl were not on the dresser. He decided to shower, drink some coffee, and then form a plan.

He stood with his eyes closed under the hot water and let the steam fill the room. The knots in his neck and shoulders were getting tighter by the day. He thought he heard something and reached for a towel as Maggie opened the door a crack.

"I brought you breakfast," she said in a cheerful voice.

"Great," he said. "Be right out."

After drying off, dressing quickly, and running his fingers through his hair, he joined her at the table near the window. She had spread out bagels, cream cheese, butter, and jam.

"I know this looks more like a New York spread than one from New Mexico, but my choices were limited. A free breakfast meant a carb breakfast, I guess."

"Hey, I'm not choosey. Thanks for going to get this." He sliced the bagel open with his knife and began to spread cream cheese on it. "What time did you leave?"

"Early," she said. "I helped Bella pack and took her down to the lobby to meet Roddy."

"She's already gone?"

"On her way home right now. I'm sure she's talking Roddy's ear off. She likes to provide a soundtrack for a road trip." Her voice took on a childish tone. "Oh, look. There's a waterfall. Did you see that fox? There are lots of ruts on this road, aren't there?" Maggie laughed and reached for a bagel.

"Does this mean we are alone in this big city and this hotel without a chaperone?"

She leaned across the table and kissed the cream cheese off his lips. "It does. And after you've finished eating, we can go back to bed for a while."

He stood and took her hand. "Breakfast can wait."

CHAPTER 28

Bella entered the hotel like a steam engine heading uphill. She huffed and puffed as her warm breath left a cold, misty trail behind her. Roddy hurried inside moments later with two suitcases and one overnight bag.

"Wait up, Bella," he said. "I've got a load here."

"You are young and strong. An old woman's luggage should not slow you down."

They rode in the elevator in silence. Bella had been gone for a week. She wasn't happy to be back, but she knew that was exactly where she needed to be. Magdalena was in big trouble, and the sooner they had a good talk, the better.

Roddy tapped on the door, and Maggie opened it. Her welcoming smile soon turned to a wary frown when she saw the look on Bella's face. "Everything all right?" she said.

"Why wouldn't it be?" Bella said. "Roddy is a good

driver, and the roads weren't too bad. We had a pleasant drive."

When Roddy came out of the bedroom where he had deposited the suitcases, Maggie said, "I can't thank you enough," and she gave him a big hug.

"No thanks needed," he said. "I enjoyed the company." His back was to Bella, and he gave Maggie a look that clearly indicated that he meant exactly the opposite of what he said.

"You need any help settling in, Bella?" Maggie said.

"I can do it by myself, thanks. I'll lie down for a little rest before I unpack."

"I'll walk you out," Maggie said to Roddy.

When they reached the elevators at the end of the hall, Maggie pushed the button for the lobby. "What was that look all about? Did she give you a hard time?"

"Let me just say that somebody got up on the wrong side of the bed this morning."

∽

AFTER BELLA WOKE up from her nap, her mood had improved, but not by much. Maggie knew that she would find out what was going on before too long. Bella seldom kept her anger, advice, or comments to herself for long. She liked to air her differences.

Bella crossed the room, sat down, and adjusted the throw pillows until she was ramrod straight. "Sit here, mija," she said and pointed to the other end of the sofa. "While I was at home, I read the cards. I know that you are keeping a dangerous secret from me."

Maggie swallowed but did not respond.

"You might as well tell me because I think I already know what it is."

"Well, if you know, why are you asking me to tell you?"

"Because telling the truth is good for the soul."

"Bella, I have not lied to you. I planned to tell you about the baby when the time was right."

"And when might that be?"

"I thought it would be better to tell Russell first. After all, he is the baby's father."

"And have you told him?"

Maggie looked ashamed. "No, not yet."

"Because?"

"Because he has too much to deal with right now. He has to relive the horrible death of his child every time the police question him."

Bella gave her a sympathetic smile. "I must ask you a question. Forgive me if you think I am trespassing on your business."

Maggie laughed nervously. "When has that ever been an issue? You have been doing that my whole life. Go ahead and ask."

Bella appeared to ignore her remark and forged ahead. "Does some small part of your heart question whether Russell was responsible for the fire? Maybe it wasn't his intention to kill anyone, but the flames got out of control?"

Maggie hesitated a moment too long before she said, "No, I have complete faith in him."

"Then, what is it, Magdalena? Why do you not tell the man you love that you are carrying his child in your belly?"

Maggie struggled with whether or not she should tell

Bella what she had been feeling, and the doubt she had been carrying around for so long.

"Tell me, child. Unburden your heart."

"Russell told me that he married Sarah because she was pregnant. Olive said Sarah trapped him, and they had nothing in common except their mutual lust. What if that's all it is with me?" she blurted out, unaware of the pain revealed in her voice.

∽

MAGGIE FELT ill enough to spend most of the afternoon in her room alternating between trips to the bathroom to throw up and short, fitful moments of sleep. She had been keeping a glass of ginger ale on her bedside table and a bag of saltine crackers tucked under the bed. She knew that some of her symptoms were associated with her pregnancy, and the guilt and indecision she felt about telling Russ the truth caused the others.

Returning from the bathroom, she pulled back the curtain and saw that the sun was sinking lower in the horizon. She wanted this day to end. Just then, her phone dinged. A text message, she thought. Maybe it was Roddy or Russ. She picked it up and saw a number that she did not recognize. Then, she read the text and had to sit down on the side of the bed to catch her breath.

TELL RUSSELL I'M SORRY. I never meant for Emma to get hurt, and her death broke my heart. I didn't know she was here at the house that night. Sarah fell and hit her head during a fight we had. It was an accident, but I set fire to the house so no one could blame me. I can't live with this guilt any longer. Please forgive me.

Hugh.

MAGGIE WANTED TO SCREAM, and cry, and scream some more. She bit her lip and rushed into Bella's room without knocking. "Bella, hurry. Get dressed. We have to go."

"What's wrong, Maggie? Tell me," she said while searching for her shoes. She had not yet dressed for bed and hurried to find her shawl and her purse.

"I have to call Russell and 9-1-1. I think Hugh is going to kill himself."

"What? Why? Why do you think that?"

"Hurry, Bella. We can talk in the truck." She rushed her grandmother out of the lobby and into the parking lot. Fortunately, the old truck started on the first try, and she put it into gear and pulled out onto the road. The streetlights were on now, and it was nearly dark.

"Where are we going?" Bella said.

"To Russell's house near the mountain."

"How do you know Hugh is there?"

"It was something he said in the text," Maggie said. "I hope I'm right, but he could be anywhere."

She drove with one hand, held her iPhone in the other, and gave Siri a command to call 911. She told the dispatcher the street name but did not know the exact address. "It's the big house near the mountain that nearly burned to the ground last year."

She swerved and almost hit the curb. "Magdalena, watch out!" her grandmother warned. "Slow down."

Maggie ignored her and said, "Hey, Siri, call Russell." She was grateful that she had entered Russell's new phone number in her contacts.

A clear female voice responded, "Calling Russell. Mobile."

The phone rang four times and then connected to voice mail. "This is Russell. Leave me a message after the tone."

"Russ, please listen to me. I got a text from Hugh, and I think he's going to kill himself. If I'm right, he's at your old house. Meet me there."

For the rest of the short drive, Maggie put both hands on the wheel and concentrated on remembering the route. When they screeched to a halt in front of the house, Maggie leaned across the seat, opened the glovebox and took out a flashlight. "Stay here," she said

"No," Bella replied. "I'm going with you."

Once inside the house, they circled the downstairs rooms and then began their ascent up the stairs to the second floor. "Hugh?" Maggie called out. "Hugh, it's Maggie. We're here to help you."

"Shh ... listen," Bella said.

Maggie heard the sirens nearing the house. She was afraid to wait for help. Even an extra moment of delay might be too late. All the doors were closed but one, so she took a chance and pushed the door open wider. As she moved the beam of the flashlight around the room, she saw a few stuffed animals and small plastic toys littering the floor.

The acrid and sour smell of gunpowder assaulted her nose, and she turned to Bella. "Do you smell that?"

"Gun," Bella said. "Be careful."

By that time, the emergency responders had reached the upper floor. "Fire Department. Call out!" a deep voice said.

"Here," Maggie shouted. "We're in here."

The lights the firefighters carried illuminated the room completely. "Over here," one of them said.

A body lay beside the frame of what had once been a bed. The two EMT's rushed to him and took his pulse. Maggie moved closer to get a better view. It was evident that Hugh was dead, and there was nothing they could do. Bloodstains and brain matter were splattered all over the wall behind him. A pistol lay on the floor beside his hand.

The men shook their heads. "He's dead, ma'am. I'm sorry."

Maggie was too shocked to respond.

"Is he related to you ladies?"

"No," Bella said. "He was nothing to us."

CHAPTER 29

When Maggie and Bella entered the small Mexican restaurant on Central Avenue, the overpowering aroma of garlic and onions made Maggie's stomach churn, and she was overcome by sudden nausea. By the time she reached the table where Russell, Roddy, and Olive sat, her face was ashen and tiny beads of sweat formed high on her forehead.

She greeted Olive and Roddy warmly and took her seat next to Russ. "I'm sorry we're late. The traffic was heavy, and I missed our exit on the freeway. I'm still learning to navigate in the big city."

Olive laughed and looked slightly bemused as she said, "Maggie, hon, it's not like we live in a huge metropolis. As far as cities go, we're pretty small, but I guess since you're from a small town, Albuquerque can be pretty intimidating. I've never been to Angel Falls, but I understand from Russ that it is charming. I'd love to come to visit sometime."

"Bella and I would like that. Maybe in the late spring

when things are slow, I'll have more time to spend with you and show you around. The weather will be cold but still comfortable enough to be outside."

"That sounds like a lovely plan." Olive cleared her throat, looked at the others and said, "I guess we're all trying to avoid the eight-hundred-pound elephant in the room?"

"No, we're not," said Maggie. "I, for one, don't want to spend one more minute of my day talking about someone who has done nothing but consume everyone's conversation." She took a sip of her water and leaned back in her chair.

"I have to agree with Maggie," Roddy said. "Hugh is dead, and tragically his note left more questions than answers. We'll never know how or why he did what he did."

"Well, the investigation is closed, right? The police have the guilty party. That seems like something to celebrate," Olive said.

Russell had been disturbingly quiet and continued to sip from his glass of amber liquid slowly. After much deliberation, when he finally spoke, he said, "Excuse me, if I can't take pleasure in the realization that my dead brother murdered my daughter." The angry retort hardened his features.

"Well, it was nice of you to pay for his cremation, and I'm really happy we didn't have to attend a service. I can't imagine how awkward that would have been," Olive said.

No one said anything and the group sitting around the table did not look at each other. Maggie noticed that Russ had signaled for another drink.

When the waiter arrived with an appetizer of nachos

and chips and salsa, the smell threatened to gag Maggie. She lightly touched Russell's sleeve and said, "I'll be right back. I need to go to the ladies' room."

"Maggie," Olive said. "Are you ill? You look awful."

Maggie covered her mouth and fled from the room as quickly as possible. Olive's eyes trailed after Maggie and then she picked up her wine glass and raised it as if for a toast. "Cheers, Russell. How absolutely marvelous for you. I'm sure you're both ecstatic."

Russell's eyes bore into Olive's. He looked confused and asked tersely, "What are you talking about?"

"Your baby, of course, I'm so happy you're going to be a father again."

∽

MAGGIE EMPTIED the contents of her stomach that, thankfully, only contained crackers and water. She supposed this is what morning sickness felt like even when it was no longer morning.

Until today, she'd had no outward symptoms of her suspected pregnancy. Oh, she'd had a little nausea that the crackers and the ginger ale took care of, but suddenly she was ravenous. She'd ordered a loaded breakfast tray of pancakes, bacon, sausage, and eggs along with juice and decaf coffee. After she removed the covering from the steaming plate and looked at all that food, it was as if she had slammed on the brakes while going a hundred miles an hour. The last thing she wanted was to eat what was on that plate.

She rolled the cart into Bella's room where her great-grandmother only clicked her tongue and shook her head.

Bella didn't say a word, but Maggie knew exactly what the old woman was thinking. *Mija, what did you think would happen? You cannot hide from the truth. Only a foolish woman waits to tell her man about his child until her body reveals the truth. Your sickness will give you away. Wait and see.*

Bella's reaction made Maggie furious, and she slammed the door. *Why did she always know everything, and why was she always right?*

Maggie knew she had waited too long. Bella had warned Maggie after she returned from her visit to Cielo Verde, that she needed to tell Russ. Maggie intended to, but she didn't want to crowd him, or even worse, pressure him into something he wasn't ready for. He had already married one woman because she was pregnant with his child and look how that turned out. Then, Hugh had killed himself and then … "Oh hell," she said.

She knew Bella was right. She should have told Russ long ago. Now, she needed to make it through this dinner and then she could tell him as soon as they were alone. She washed her face and hands and pinched her cheeks trying to get some color back.

The dining room was noisy with the clanking of silver and the hum of voices. When she reached the table, she stopped short. Russ was sitting at the table by himself. "Where did everyone go?" Maggie said looking around the room.

"I sent Olive home, and I asked Roddy to take Bella back to the hotel." His voice was low and controlled. "Get your coat, Magdalena. We're leaving."

"But, why? What's the matter?"

"Do you really want to talk about it here in this restaurant with strangers listening?"

Maggie was confused until she looked into his eyes. She saw anger, but more than that, she saw disappointment. She let him help her into her coat, and they walked out the door. He knows, she thought, and he isn't happy.

He took her elbow and guided her in the opposite direction from where she had parked the truck. "Where are we going? I parked back there." She stopped and pointed.

He continued to pull her along until they reached his company vehicle. He opened the passenger door and said, "Get in, Magdalena. I'll take you back to the hotel."

It was only a short drive, and if it hadn't been so cold outside, she could easily have walked. She opened her mouth several times to speak but stopped herself each time. When he was ready to talk, he would. She'd never seen Russell angry, but she was pretty sure that at this moment, fury was the emotion that was oozing from every pore.

The shops and restaurants flew by, and in minutes they were in front of the Hyatt. He pulled into an empty parking space and put the car in park. The only sounds were the heat blowing on their feet and the whine of traffic from the road.

"How long have you known? And don't play games with me and say, known what? It's pretty obvious that you're pregnant. Who else knows besides Olive? Of course, Bella does. Did you tell Roddy too?"

"No, of course not. Why would I tell Roddy?"

"Maybe for the same reason you didn't tell me."

"What are you implying?" Maggie said. She looked as if he had slapped her. "Are you suggesting that Roddy and I—"

"I didn't mean anything by that, Maggie," he interrupted. "You've thrown me a curve, and I don't know what to think."

"I haven't told anyone. Bella knows, but that's because she's Bella."

"Stupid me then. I've only been sleeping with you in every intimate way possible, and I never suspected."

He turned to her then and raised his voice. Something he'd never done before. "How long have you known?"

"Since the morning after we made love for the first time, I just knew."

"And you didn't think it was important to tell me, the baby's father? I am the father, aren't I, Magdalena? How can I ever trust you again?"

Maggie blinked, and tears filled her eyes. She grabbed the door handle and tried to get out of the car.

"I'm sorry. I didn't mean that. You know I didn't mean that. Please don't leave."

Maggie spoke through her tears. "I didn't tell you at first because I wasn't sure, then you were accused of murder, and I didn't want to complicate things, and then when I found out the reason you married Sarah, I didn't want you to think I was trying to trap you."

Russell reached for her, but she dodged his hand and was successful in her escape. "I need to go in now, Russ. Before we both say things we can never take back. I love you, and yes, I'm going to have your baby whether you forgive me or not. I know trust is hard for you, and I'm so sorry that I've broken that trust."

"Magdalena, it's so unfair that I had to find out from Olive. How could you do that to me?"

"I'm going to go back home, Russ, back where I

belong. We can talk later after we've both had time to think," Maggie said.

Maggie waited a brief moment for Russell to say something, anything. When he didn't, she got out of the car and shut the door. She hurried toward the entrance of the hotel and opened the heavy glass door. When she got inside the warm lobby, she turned and looked back hoping to see that Russ had followed her. But the circular drive was empty, and he was gone.

CHAPTER 30

Maggie had a miserable, sleepless night. With every little sound she heard in the corridor, she hoped it was Russ, but he had never returned to the hotel, and his phone went straight to voice mail when she called him that morning.

The last thing he said was, "How could you do that to me?"

Had she lost the man she loved? Was not telling him about the baby for his protection, or was she being selfish and thinking only of herself?

She was worried about Russ. He had been so angry with her last night, and he had taken Hugh's suicide hard. He was pulling back into himself and becoming the man he was before they met. Then, she made it worse for him when he found out about the baby. She wanted to believe that he would forgive her, and that she and Bella could pull him through the crisis, but this morning she was having serious doubts.

So many people he had trusted and loved had deliberately betrayed him and told him lies. How does someone get over that? How could he ever trust anyone again?

Thanksgiving was only a few weeks away, and Maggie wanted to get back home as soon as possible. It had been a stressful and tumultuous week, and she hoped never to have one like it again. Hugh's suicide was an ending to an even more tragic crime of passion. Russell blamed himself for allowing Hugh into little Emma's life, and he was torn between hating Hugh and feeling sorry for his brother, the little boy he'd grown up with.

Maggie had no such feelings. She loathed the man and had barely tolerated being in the same room with Hugh since the first time they'd met. He'd used Russell's feelings for Emma to provide himself with an alibi. The murders had been premeditated and cruel. The man was evil, and she was glad he was dead.

While she was at it, she also detested Sarah, a woman she had never met. God might throw lightning bolts her way because of these thoughts, but she didn't care. The selfish woman ruined three lives and was indirectly responsible for her own child's death. She had tried to destroy Russell, a man who had been nothing but good to her.

Her thoughts continued to race. No wonder she couldn't sleep. And to put the cherry on the cake, Bella had been behaving strangely. When Maggie asked her what was wrong, Bella simply said, "I don't know. Something. But you need to take care of your own house before you mess with mine."

Bella had warned her that keeping the baby a secret was the wrong thing to do, but Maggie didn't want Russ to feel compelled to commit to their relationship permanently. Now, look at the mess she had created by ignoring her great-grandmother's advice.

Maggie pulled her suitcase out of the closet and began packing it with the clothes she'd brought from home when she heard the ring of the hotel phone. Who in the world can that be, she thought? It wouldn't be Russell; he'd call her cell. She missed stubbing her toe on the bed by mere inches on her mad dash to stop the ringing. Bella was resting, and she didn't want the noise to wake her.

"Hello," she said breathlessly.

"Oh, Maggie. I'm so glad I got you. I was afraid you'd be gone."

"What do you mean? Gone where?"

"Home, back to Angel Falls." The voice was thick and unsteady.

"Olive? Is that you? What's wrong?"

"It's Russ. When he was at the office today, he was so out of sorts. Not like himself at all. I'm sure you've noticed."

"Yes, he's been upset and rightly so."

"He left the office, and I followed him. Maybe I shouldn't have, but I was concerned. The roads are icy, and he was driving so fast I could barely keep up with him. He's here at his old house. Maggie, I'm terrified he's going to do something. He won't let me in the room, and I don't know what to do. I can't call the police. Think of the publicity."

Maggie sighed with exasperation. "Olive, if you're worried about him, publicity is the last thing you should be concerned about. I'm not sure what you mean by *do something*. What are you afraid he will do?"

"I ... I ... don't know, but he'll listen to you. He's saying all of these crazy things. Can you come to help me? Help him?"

"I'll be there as fast as I can," Maggie said. Her heart was beating a mile a minute.

"I've got to get back to him," Olive said. "I can't talk anymore. I'm going to try to get into the room. Please come quickly and be careful."

Maggie wrote a short note to Bella telling her where she was going, grabbed her keys and purse, and ran out the door. Thankful that Roddy had returned her truck from the restaurant the night before, she jumped into the driver's seat. Praying he would answer, and she could talk him down from anything he had planned, she called Russell's cell one more time. Again, it went to voice mail. "Please, Russ. Talk to me. I love you. I'm on my way to your old house. Please wait for me."

Sleet fell from the dark and cloudy sky and hit the windshield as she pulled out of the parking garage. She'd forgotten to bring a coat, and she shivered as the old red truck whined when she shifted gears. Why didn't she ever check weather reports?

She'd only been to Russ's old house twice, once with Olive, and again with Bella. She was unfamiliar with the city and hoped she could locate the correct street. The sleet intensified, and she could feel the temperature dropping.

Getting to Russ was all she could think about. If all the bad things that had happened to him had come crashing in at once, she knew she had to get to him fast. She needed to tell him how much she and his baby needed him and how much he was loved.

THE RINGING PHONE woke Bella from a troubled, dream-filled sleep. For a moment, she felt disoriented and wasn't quite sure where she was. When the hotel room came into focus, she remembered she was in Albuquerque and not in her bed at home. Something was wrong. Last night she had felt uneasy, but this morning her sense of danger had intensified.

She reached for her cards that she kept on the bedside table and spread them across the fluffy comforter. Bella had lived through her share of tragedies over the years: the death of her beloved husband, one son killed in a war, another died of a failing heart, and a granddaughter lost to an aggressive form of leukemia. Bella wasn't able to predict the future and could not change someone's fate, as she well knew with her own family. Sometimes, however, by knowing the present and what was going on around her, she could see conflicts, emotions, and danger that affected the future.

She turned over the first of the five cards she'd drawn from the deck. She saw Despair, but she chose to wait for the other cards before she panicked. Then she turned over Desolation, Betrayal, and Duplicity. When she turned over the final card, she rose from the bed and rushed into the sitting room. "Magdalena?" she called out. Her voice was fraught with terror.

She pushed open Maggie's door and saw the open suitcase half-filled with clothes. "Maggie, where are you?" she yelled again fighting panic as she hurried back into the sitting room. Then, she saw the note lying on the small table. When she picked it up, she took in the rushed scribble of Maggie's handwriting, and her eyes widened with fear.

∼

Maggie finally found the house after several aggravating wrong turns. The temperature had dropped rapidly, and the sleet changed to heavy snowflakes the closer she traveled toward the mountain. The house looked eerie and foreboding like something from a Charlotte Brontë novel.

Thankful for her rubber-soled shoes, she fought to keep her balance as she ran up the slick walkway toward the boarded-up entrance. "Russell? Olive? Where are you?" she called out as she stepped inside. When she got no answer, she shouted again, "Where are you?"

"Up here," she heard Olive call. "He's in the bedroom. Hurry."

Maggie rushed up the stairs unsure of Russell's condition. She was confused, scared, and frustrated. *What the hell was the man doing?* she thought.

She charged into the room only to see the French doors that led to the balcony falling off their hinges with most of the glass broken. The wind whipped the falling snow onto the deck swishing the shredded window remnants into the frigid air.

She looked around wildly and heard the door slam behind her, and as she turned, she saw Olive calmly leaning against it. "Olive? Where's Russ? What's going on?"

"He left. I couldn't get him to stay. He asked me to talk to you."

"But you said he was here. A moment ago, when I was downstairs, you said he was up here with you in the bedroom."

"Yes, he went out that way on the balcony." Olive placed her hand on Maggie's back and moved her toward the open air.

Maggie stopped as an unnatural stab of fear pricked at her spine. She turned and looked into Olive's wide, feral eyes and saw a cunning look spread across her face. Maggie took two steps back and stopped when she felt a knife against her ribs.

The nausea that had been blessedly absent most of the day returned in full force and with it the knowledge that she was about to die. How could she have been so naïve? How could she not have seen it? "*You*," Maggie whispered.

She felt the point of the knife cut through her cotton sweater and instinctively moved her hand to protect her child. Olive yanked the weapon upward slicing the tips of Maggie's fingers, and Maggie yelped and pulled her hand away.

"Where's Russell? What have you done to him?"

Olive laughed, and her voice rang hollow in the room devoid of furniture and with only remnants of scattered objects from a previous life.

"I would never harm Russell. I love him. I'll be there to comfort him like I should have been the last time. How was I supposed to know he would disappear and find you?"

"Please," Maggie took another step back. "I'm going to have a baby. I'll leave. I'll leave today and never see him again. Please don't kill my baby."

"You stupid, stupid woman. You're nothing but an

inconvenience. You and Russell have nothing in common. This thing you think you have with him would have fizzled and died. But when I realized you'd managed to trick him in the same way Sarah did, I knew I had to act."

"I didn't trick him, although I'm sure he thinks I did. He hates me now." Maggie backed up another step. "You'll see. I'll go back home, and he'll stay here with you where he belongs."

"He would never let you. You are carrying his child. He would gladly sacrifice himself again for this child. Don't you know anything about him? He would move to that ridiculous place in the mountains and give up his creative genius to muck out horse stalls and build cabins."

"He told you that?"

"Of course, he told me that. He wants a happy family, and I will give him what he wants and what he needs. It will take a little time, but he will get over your tragic accident, and we'll go on. After I give him a child, he will forget all about you."

Maggie's mind was frantically considering all her options. She could rush Olive and try to get the knife, but the woman was at least twenty pounds heavier and several inches taller. She could try to run, but she had nowhere to go—a balcony behind her and a closed door in front. The only thing to do was to try and buy time hoping against hope that Russ had heard her message.

"Why did you kill Sarah?" Maggie said. "She was going to leave him and take Emma. Wasn't that what you wanted? To have him all to yourself?"

"Because she would have always been there in his life. I wanted them gone. It should always have been Russell and me from the beginning. He would have chosen me if Sarah hadn't tempted him."

Maggie didn't agree. She knew from their conversations that Russell had been deeply attracted to Sarah and may even have been in love with her, and he would have never slept with her if he had romantic feelings for Olive.

"They'll know you murdered me. How do you ever expect to get away with it?"

"It won't be difficult. I'm Russell's trusted friend, and because of my loyalty to him, I was also your friend. Why would there even be a reason to suspect foul play?" Olive pushed the knife against Maggie and forced her to continue to move backward. "You and Russell had a terrible fight, and you went looking for him. Unable to find him you came to his old home thinking he might be here."

She moved Maggie forcefully toward the balcony doors, and the icy wind blew against her back. Maggie shivered from the cold and fright. Olive was insane, and Maggie was beginning to realize she was probably going to die. How she died would be up to her.

"You'll simply have a terrible accident. You came out onto the balcony looking for Russell. The railing was faulty from the fire damage, and tragically you fell over onto the concrete below."

Maggie stopped and resisted Olive's advances and the sting of the knife against her. "I won't cooperate. You may kill me, but it won't look like an accident. You'll have to cut me to pieces with that knife. What if it doesn't work out the way you planned? What if the police suspect Russell as they did in Sarah and Emma's deaths? As you said, we had a terrible fight. Roddy knows, and so does Bella. What will you do then?"

"Don't underestimate me, Maggie. I've got a few more smarts than a simple country girl like you. I found a patsy last time in Hugh. I imagine if it comes to that I can find one again. I'm pretty sure I can get the authorities to believe there was something between you and Roddy. As for Bella," Olive waved her free hand in the air, "she is an old woman. What harm can she do me?"

They were outside on the deck now, and Maggie could hear the wind whistling against the side of the house. If she was going to take a stand, it would have to be soon. "Did you kill Hugh, or did he really kill himself?"

Olive threw her head back and laughed into the wind. "What do you think? I merely helped him with a decision he'd been contemplating. Hugh was overcome with guilt for having betrayed his brother after Russell had been so good to him. And as for your idea that no one will believe it was an accident, I'm afraid your poor body will be so destroyed from the fall that a knife wound will hardly be noticed after the building debris falls on you. I've fixed it so that when you go over the edge, the railing and half of the side of the building will go with you."

Olive thrust the knife into Maggie's side and pulled the blade out to stab her again when the bedroom door flew open, and an apparition with long, silver hair bounded into the room with a scream on her lips. "Get away from my Maggie."

Maggie managed to pull away toward the outside wall when Olive turned to confront her attacker while backing away toward the rail. Olive failed to see the small child's toy that had not been there before, lying innocently on the deck, and her foot caught and rolled, forcing her off balance as she slammed into the rail. Her shrill screams split the cold, night air as Maggie saw her tumble over and downward and watched as the building crumbled.

Bella reached Maggie in a matter of seconds and pulled her away from the edge as Maggie's lifeblood flowed onto the old woman.

CHAPTER 31

Searching for Magdalena, Russ moved his hand around under the covers. He frowned, mumbled, and pulled the blanket up under his chin. He was cold and was searching for her body heat.

His eyes popped open, and a strange feeling of déjà vu came over him as he looked around the room. He was fully dressed and lying on a living room sofa. He sat up and immediately recognized his surroundings. He was at Olive's house, but he wasn't quite sure how he got there.

He remembered the argument with Magdalena clearly. He'd watched her, with his heart in his throat, as she walked back into the hotel lobby. He'd been angry, hurt, and confused. He should have followed her in. Why didn't he? Instead, he'd driven to his office so that he could wallow a little in self-pity.

Olive had come into the room. He remembered that. He'd accused her of knowing about Magdalena's pregnancy and keeping things from him again. Olive had assured him she'd been as surprised as he was when

Maggie went running to the ladies' room. That's when she figured out that Maggie was pregnant. Funny, he hadn't even considered that possibility until Olive made her toast.

Why was he here? What the hell had happened? "Olive," he called out. When he got no answer, he got up, raised his voice and called her again. She'd fixed him a drink, and on top of the three he'd consumed earlier he recalled a mind-numbing feeling and then little else.

Magdalena will be worried and hurt, no doubt, he thought. He searched his pockets and mumbled, "Where the hell is my phone?"

He frantically searched under the couch cushions to no avail. It was gloomy outside, and he could hear the wind blowing against the front window. He was relieved to see Olive's car parked in the driveway partially covered in fresh snow that was continuing to pile up on the sidewalks and lawn. *When had it started to snow?* he wondered. *Maybe he was still asleep and dreaming.*

Calling Olive's name, he continued to search for his phone as he walked from room to room. She was nowhere in sight. His wallet was in his pocket, and so were his keys, but his car was not parked outside. Maybe Olive had taken it? He shook his head clearing his thoughts, "No, stupid. You have the keys."

He got on his knees and decided to give the sofa one more look and was rewarded with a shiny gleam among the dust bunnies. "There you are."

When he pulled his phone out, the screen was filled with texts, missed calls, and voice messages. Most of the missed calls were from Magdalena, and the last one was from Bella.

His fingers shook as he swiped to listen to Bella's message. Something had happened to Magdalena. The baby? It had to be. Why else would she call? He was alarmed when he heard Bella's strong, lilting voice say, *"You stupid boy. Where are you? My girl is in trouble, and I'm going there now."*

Where is there? The hospital. Was she losing the baby? He started to call her back but decided to listen to Magdalena's last message first. He listened to it twice to make sure he had heard her correctly. It didn't make any sense. Why was she going to his old house? She apparently thought he was going to do something foolish and was genuinely concerned because he could hear the panic in her voice.

Russell, Olive, and Darren all lived in close proximity. It had made it easy when they needed to conference in person, and rather than go to the office they would meet at Russell's home. His house was one street over and a few blocks down from this one. He hadn't been back to the house since the fire, and the only person who could force him to do so was Magdalena.

He called her number, and after several rings, the call went to voice mail. He rushed out the front door and sprinted down the snow-packed street that thankfully was not slick. He punched the return call for Bella. His lungs burned as he sucked in the freezing air. What Bella said made his heart stop.

∽

HE COULD SEE FLASHING lights from the ambulance and police cars as he rounded the corner and ran past them forcing his way into the house and up the stairs. He came to an abrupt stop when he saw Magdalena's small form surrounded by medical professionals. Bella was talking to a uniformed officer off to the side. She looked up as he approached.

"Bella?" he said. Fear gripped his gut as he moved toward the stretcher. An oxygen mask covered Magdalena's face, and he was only able to grasp and squeeze her hand before the EMT's rushed her out of the room. He followed them out to the ambulance only to have the door shut in his face with a terse, "Let's roll."

He stood bewildered as he heard the loud wail of the siren and watched the lights turn onto the main road. "Mr. Zarek," a young officer said, "I understand this is your home?"

"What? Yes, it is." His face clouded with uneasiness. "I have to go to the hospital. I have to go. Where's Bella? We have to go?"

"Mr. Zarek, I need to ask you a few questions."

"I don't have a car. How will I get there?"

"Mr. Zarek, are you all right?"

"What happened? Will she be okay?"

Bella and another policeman walked out of the house and joined them. "Russell," Bella said. "This nice young man will take us to the hospital. We need to be with Maggie."

"Will you please tell me what happened?"

"Olive is dead. She tried to kill Maggie. I will tell you all I know on the way."

RUSSELL AND BELLA sat side-by-side on the surprisingly comfortable seats in the critical care waiting room of UNM Hospital. Except for an elderly couple, they were the only occupants. It seemed like they'd been there forever, but when Russell looked at his watch, it had only been for a little over an hour.

A worried looking Roddy joined. He had two cups of Starbucks coffee in his hands and a folded blanket under his arm. He knelt in front of Bella, and Russell took the blanket and draped the warmth across the old woman's thin shoulders. Russell knew Bella was barely holding it together, but someone who had never been around her wouldn't know.

She fiercely grasped his hand, the blue veins clearly visible through her transparent skin and said, "Don't feel guilty—either of you. Olive was a crazy woman. How can anyone foresee crazy? How could you know?"

Tears glistened in her eyes, but her voice was strong and firm when she said, "She will live. I know this."

Russell squeezed her hand and said, "You knew."

Russell heard the footfall in the hall and was surprised to see Detective Flores. "What's he doing here?"

"I called him," Roddy said.

"Mrs. Morales, Mr. Zarek," Flores nodded and then moved a chair close to them. "How is she?"

"We don't know. Maggie's in surgery, and the doctor said it would be a least a couple of hours. They won't know how much damage was done until they get ... well ... until they take a look."

"As I understand it," he said looking at Bella, "you found her in Russell's house in a struggle with Olive Greeley."

"Crazy woman had a knife and was going to shove my little girl over the rail. She stabbed her, and if I hadn't arrived when I did, she would have been successful. She slipped when I arrived and went over instead." Bella shook her head and sighed, "Evil, evil woman."

"Was your granddaughter able to tell you why?"

"All she said was …" She stopped and composed her response. "All she said, that you need to know, is that Olive killed Sarah and Emma, and then made Hugh's death look like a suicide."

Detective Flores looked at Russell and appeared to be waiting for a comment. When he didn't say anything, the detective said, "Why would she do that?"

Russell raked his fingers through his hair and shook his head, "God, I don't know. Evidently, she had some insane idea that she and I belonged together, and everyone I loved was a threat."

"Were you lovers?"

"No, never," Russell bit out the words.

"The investigation will need to be reopened because of these new developments. I'm sorry this has happened. I liked Ms. Morales very much."

"Liked?" Roddy said. "She's in surgery; she's alive."

"I meant no disrespect. Poor choice of words. Please let me know when she is out of surgery and can answer questions."

Both men stared as Flores left the room.

"What was that about, Roddy? Does he think I know something?" Russell said.

"I have no idea. But I'm going to find out."

Maggie was sleeping peacefully, and so it seemed was Bella. There was a large recliner in the room, and after much prodding, Russell had finally convinced Bella to take a short nap.

When Magdalena's eyelids fluttered, he immediately moved closer to the bed and stroked her hand. Hey, sleepyhead. You're awake."

"She grimaced, and her first thought was Emma. "The baby? Is the …"

"The baby is fine. The OB said it has a strong heartbeat, and your surgeon said you are one tough lady. He'll be in later tonight to explain everything to you, but he said you would make a full recovery."

"Russ, I'm so sorry I didn't tell you. I didn't try to trick you."

He smoothed her hair back from her head and kissed her lightly on the forehead. "It doesn't matter now, okay? You're going to be fine, and the baby is fine. We can talk about this later when you're stronger."

"Bella saved my life."

"Yes, she did. She's a remarkable woman and pretty feisty for eighty-five. I'm sure she won't let us forget it."

"I heard that," Bella said as she stretched and sat up, "And I'm way too old to be doing it again, so you need to choose your friends wisely."

"How did you know?"

"The cards, mija. It's all about the cards."

CHAPTER 32

"Where's Bella?" Maggie asked after looking around the hospital room and finding the recliner empty.

"I finally got her to agree to let Roddy take her back to the hotel for a proper nap.

She complained but finally agreed. She's a little worn out. How are you feeling?" Russ asked, pulling his chair up to the bed.

"Have you been here all night? Talk about worn out; you look exhausted."

"I'm okay. I got a couple of winks."

"Russ," Maggie said reaching for his hand. "We need to talk. I think …"

There was a soft rap on the door, and Detective Flores and Roddy walked in. "I told the detective I wanted to be present for any conversations he had with any of you. Is this a good time?"

Maggie nodded, sighed and said, "Yes, I guess it will have to be. I need to get it over with."

"I've already spoken to Mrs. Morales, with her attorney present. We won't be looking at any charges."

"What do you mean charges?" Maggie said sitting up in the bed and wincing. "Olive was going to kill me, and Bella didn't touch that woman. It's a miracle that she had the presence of mind to call for a taxi. She saved my life."

"Yes, ma'am, I understand, but I had to look at all of the facts. Do you have a problem if I record this conversation?"

Maggie looked at Roddy, and he nodded his agreement. "Yes, fine."

For the next half hour, Flores asked questions and Maggie and Russell answered them, although Russell had no facts about the actual incident and little memory of why he was at Olive's house.

"Here's what we know so far from looking at the scene and going through Olive's phone records. This information also goes to what we believe happened in the deaths of your wife and daughter, Mr. Zarek. We had already established that Sarah was dead before the fire was set. Your daughter died of smoke inhalation, and we don't know if she was a target, or if Olive Greeley did not intend for her to die. Looking at Russell he said, "Sadly, it looks like that was her intent."

Maggie felt Russell's grip on her hand intensify, but that was his only reaction. He'd been holding so much emotion in since she'd been hurt, and she knew he needed to let it out.

"Olive Greeley started the fire from a phone application. She was sharp enough to get access to your account and was able to monitor everything in your home including your alarm system, your cameras, and your heating system as well. She simply let the gas fumes build up, and then she remotely set off the explosion with a spark from an appliance."

He shifted his gaze to Russell and said, "Now you can see why you were our prime suspect. Then, when your brother came through with an alibi saying that you were together, that blew our theory out of the water. Especially, after we found out you were drunk and had passed out at the time the fire started."

"What about Hugh? Did he really kill himself?"

"From your statement, Ms. Morales, we know that Hugh was innocent of the murders. Olive didn't admit to composing the confession text, but it stands to reason that she did. We found records of a phone call from Olive to Hugh the day of his death. We'll never know how she got him to your house, Russell, or how she was able to make it look like a suicide. But if it is any consolation, which I'm sure it isn't, your brother wasn't involved in your family's murders, and I believe he was genuinely sorry for his involvement with your wife."

Flores turned off the recorder and stood. "I'm sorry if I was hard on you, Russell. I follow the leads where they take me. I'm glad it wasn't you at the end."

"Detective?" Russell said. "Do you think she drugged me?"

"Most likely, since your last recollection was Olive Greeley giving you a drink at the office. Since she left you drugged at her house and walked to your former home to meet Ms. Morales, she was planning to use you as an alibi in case you or she were ever questioned. She didn't take your size into account and didn't give you a big enough dose, so you woke up before you were supposed to. Again, as I said, we'll never really know."

Roddy walked with him out into the hallway and Maggie could hear a muffled conversation but couldn't make out what was said.

Russell had turned a pale shade of gray, and he breathed in shallow gasps.

"Russ, are you okay?" Maggie said.

"I ... I need to get out ... I need to breathe. I'll be back later," Russell released her hand and practically ran Roddy down as he came back into the room.

"Whoa, where's he going in such a hurry?" Roddy asked.

Tears blinded Maggie's eyes and choked her voice. "Anywhere but here."

~

RUSSELL COULDN'T GET out of the hospital fast enough. He got in Maggie's truck and drove until he noticed a sign for San Felipe Pueblo and realized he was halfway to Santa Fe. He pulled over at the closest truck stop and stared out at the cars driving up I-25. He knew he had to go back soon to face Maggie. She wanted to talk, but he was afraid to listen.

Everything was his fault. So many people were dead, and all because of him. He didn't love Sarah enough to give her the exciting life she wanted, and that made her turn to other men. Then, even worse, he put his trust in a man he believed to be his friend when he knew from the beginning what type of person Darren was. He had opened the door and said, "Come on in, take my wife. I'm too busy making money."

What kind of a man was he that Magdalena who had the purest heart and most honest soul was afraid to tell him she was pregnant? He'd yelled at her and suggested that the baby might not be his. How could she ever forgive him? How could he ever forgive himself?

And then there was Olive. How could he ever forgive himself for misjudging Olive? He'd never known. Never even suspected. She'd killed his little girl all because of him, and she had almost killed Magdalena.

Magdalena would be so much better off without him in her life. He knew he would only let her and the baby down. He didn't want to love her, and he didn't want to be responsible for her happiness. He was not brave enough to take another chance on losing the people he loved.

He wanted to ask Bella for guidance, but he was afraid of what she might say. He didn't want to know or to hear her words. He wanted to keep running without a backward glance, but he had to say goodbye. He owed that to Magdalena.

It was past midnight when Russ got back to the hospital room. The lights were dim, but he could see that she was alone. The only sounds were the constant beeps from the monitors.

He stood over her, gazing down into her beautiful face and was not surprised when she opened her eyes. "You came back," she said in a whisper.

"Yes," he said and ran his fingers down her cheek caressing her face. "I'll stay until you are better."

"And then?" she said in a choked voice.

He couldn't look her in the eyes, and his shoulders sagged.

"Russ, when they let me out of here, Bella and I are going home to Cielo Verde where we belong. If you're not coming with us, there's no need to hang around."

A pain squeezed his heart, and he hesitated for one brief moment before he turned and quietly left the room.

CHAPTER 33

Maggie pulled the curtain back and marveled at the beautiful snowdrifts and fresh powder blanketing the ground. For the first time in two years, the snowpack was going to be perfect for winter playtime, and the new website Russ had designed for Cielo Verde had paid off. Guests from all around the country were signing up, and reservations for the Christmas season and beyond were nearing capacity.

Two weeks earlier, she and Bella had invited Roddy and his parents to Thanksgiving dinner, and Dora and Billy Hansen had handled most of the cooking and all of the grocery shopping. "You need to take it easy, so that little one will grow healthy and strong," Dora said. She was even worse than Bella about being a mother hen.

Maggie knew her limits. She would never do anything to jeopardize the health of her baby, but, at the same time, it was not in her nature to sit and knit booties. She had always been an outdoor girl, even in winter, and being pregnant could not change that.

She cradled her belly protectively with her hand as she made her way across the yard to the barn. Billy took care of any lifting, including the heavy hay bales, but she was perfectly capable of feeding and watering the horses, and she enjoyed doing it.

God had blessed her recovery, and her injuries were healing well. She still wore leather gloves while working with the horses because on her left hand the tips of the fingers that the knife had sliced were healed, but tender. The doctor had told her that it was possible her damaged nerves would always be sensitive.

Since Lyman's big construction project had come to a screeching halt after he got arrested, Maggie didn't have to go looking for wranglers to work the horses, and guides to entertain the guests. Men in desperate need of winter jobs were knocking on her door. She could take her pick.

Everything about her financial future seemed to be improving, but her personal life was still a mess. In a couple of weeks, she could learn her baby's gender, if she wanted to, but Maggie knew that would be a waste of time. In her heart, she had known since the child's conception that the baby was a girl. A girl who embodied the spirit of another little girl named Emma. Believing that this child would always be connected to Russ's little Emma, made her both sad and hopeful.

At the same time, it made her ache for Russell. She understood why he had left her, and she took full responsibility for driving him away. So many people had betrayed his trust, and it hurt her to know that she was among them. His words still haunted her, but she knew they were true. *"How can I ever trust you again?"*

Bella had not attempted to foretell the future, and Maggie had no intention of asking her to do a reading or make a prediction. She loved Russell with all of her heart, and she wanted him to be there for his child and wanted the three of them to make a life together. Knowing that what she wanted and what would come to pass might be very different, she resolved to stay strong.

She was Bella Marie Morales' great-granddaughter and Connie Morales' daughter. She would be the third woman in succession to be courageous, independent, and brave. She wanted her man, wanted him desperately, but if he never returned, she would be an example for her daughter and carry on and make a good life without him.

∽

MAGGIE'S FOOTSTEPS crunched in the snow as she walked out of the barn. A white jeep with the sheriff's logo and red beacon lights on the top sat in the driveway. She recognized the deputy and made her way toward him with a little apprehension. The last time the law had been in her driveway it was to pick up Russell.

"Hello, ma'am. I'm not sure if you remember me. I'm Jonas Clearwater," he said reaching out to shake her hand.

"Of course, I do, but it's been awhile. Is something the matter?"

"Until Buck was put on leave, I was mostly working on the far end of the county. Looks like that situation is going to turn into something more permanent, so they brought me back to serve as the temporary sheriff until they hold a new election."

"Oh, yes, I'd heard Buck had been put on suspension. I

can't say that I'm sorry. He wasn't much of a lawman. No offense to your profession."

"Oh, none taken, ma'am. He left that impression on a lot of folks. I've been in contact with the FBI and I wanted to let you and Ms. Bella know what they said."

"FBI?" Maggie said, clearly confused. "Let's walk on up to the house and get out of the cold, and you can talk to Bella too."

The house was warm, and Maggie could hear the crackle of the fire Dora had started earlier that morning. Bella walked out of the kitchen with two cups of coffee as if she had been expecting company and placed the mugs on the large dining table.

"Jonas Clearwater," she said.

Maggie saw the amazement on the deputy's face and wanted to laugh but picked up the cup of coffee from the table instead.

"I saw you outside. I figured you'd be coming inside, and it's cold." She pointed to the coffee. "Please sit down."

"How do you know who I am?"

"Your father. You look just like him. How's his back these days?"

"His back?" the man said, now more confused than ever. "He had surgery about a month ago. He's doing well. I didn't know you were in contact with my dad."

Maggie could see where this was going and headed it off before the poor man decided to run screaming from the house. Bella could do that to some people. The older she got the more cantankerous she became. She enjoyed playing games way too much.

"Bella, Deputy Clearwater, or I guess it's Sheriff Clearwater now, has been in contact with the FBI. He came to talk to us about what they said."

"Yes, ma'am," he said pulling his hat from his head and transferring it back and forth between each hand. "The Bureau is investigating a group of men with headquarters in Nevada. Especially one man who has been pressuring landowners to sell their property."

"That would be us," Maggie said. "I was trying to get the sheriff to take me seriously and I know Lyman O'Dell was in the thick of it. Thankfully we were able to come up with the money to keep afloat," she said giving Bella a soft smile.

"Lyman's in serious hot water with the feds. Bank robbery and racketeering seem to be the main charges. He started singing like a canary after he figured out the feds weren't going to give him a deal. I guess he thought he had some big ace in the hole, you know, after giving them the info on that rich guy that was living here."

"That didn't work out so well for him, I hear," Maggie said.

"No, not so well. They didn't give him a deal, but after a little extra pressure, he gave up the name of the big fish. Unfortunately, without any proof they don't have enough evidence to bring any charges against the fella yet. It's Lyman's word against his."

"And Marty?" Bella said. "Who's going to pay for killing Marty?"

"According to Lyman, he didn't have anything to do with that. Marty caught the guys trying to vandalize your property, and they got rid of him. Lyman said they were the same two fellas that were found dead after setting the fire here."

Clearwater took out a card and handed it to Bella. "This is the name of the special agent in charge of the investigation. He said to give him a call if you had more information or if you had questions. He says Lyman's going to go away for a long time," he looked at Bella. "I know that won't bring Marty Chavez back, but at least he will get a little bit of justice."

"Thank you for coming out here to tell us this in person. We appreciate the kindness." Bella touched the man gently on his arm and said, "I saw your father in town a while ago. That's how I know about his back."

The relief on the man's face was almost comical, and Maggie shot Bella a knowing look. Maggie had been with Bella the few times they'd been to town recently, and her great-grandmother hadn't spoken with anyone.

As they watched Sheriff Clearwater walk to his car, Maggie hugged Bella and kissed her tenderly on the check.

"I love you, Bella. Life with you is never dull."

"Well, I thought the young man was going to faint, and after he started talking, I decided I liked him. I didn't want to scare him away."

~

WITHOUT WARNING, three days before Christmas, a series of avalanches began in the high country in New Mexico. The rain falling on snow, the strong winds, and a warming trend had produced dangerous conditions. Many of the ski areas were closed for safety, and residents of the mountainous areas were told to be on high alert.

Maggie and her staff worked tirelessly to ensure that

her guests were safe, and the local forest ranger came to the lodge to give a safety talk to everyone at Cielo Verde.

"We are seeing slides where none have ever been before," he said. There's no need to be afraid, but by all means, do not wander far from your cabin and do not go near the base of the mountain." There was loud murmuring, and then the questions began.

"Can we get out of here and drive back to Albuquerque?"

"Yes, but not today. The highway department is working to clear the road of snow."

"You mean the road is blocked?"

He nodded. "I'm afraid so."

"How long will that take?"

"It depends on whether or not we get another slide. If we don't, then you should be good to go by tomorrow noon."

He stood and fingered his hat in his hand. "If you ask me, I think you should stay put and have a great Christmas at this beautiful lodge like you planned. Then, after Christmas, you can take a look at the weather and make your plans."

Maggie made her way to the front of the room. "We have plenty of food, the cabins are stocked with firewood, and Christmas Eve is tomorrow night." She smiled and hoped that she looked confident. In truth, she was concerned that if there was a power outage, she did not have enough backup generators to keep all the cabins lit.

∼

After the ranger left, Maggie went into the kitchen to talk to Dora. "I'm not telling you to be stingy, but we should cut back on the portions and the number of side dishes that we serve with each meal to save on food. We may make it to the store in a couple of days, but who knows? A few of these people look like they could be mean if they're hungry."

Her joke fell flat, and she sat down near Bella. "Are you okay?" she asked her grandmother.

"I'm fine, mija. I have seen winters like these many times in my years. Spring will come again."

"Is that a prediction or merely a statement to calm me?"

"It is the truth. If you are stressed, that could harm your baby."

"I know that, Bella," Maggie snapped. "What do you suggest I do about it?"

∽

Christmas Eve and Christmas Day both turned out great. The guests seemed to forget that they were trapped at the lodge, as they ate, danced, opened gifts, and sang carols. But the next day, Maggie got a call from the DMV telling her that yet another slide blocked the only road out of Cielo Verde. They were working tirelessly to clear it, and they would call her back as soon as the news was better.

Maggie pictured an empty refrigerator and cold cabins and angry guests pounding on her door. Suddenly, she felt like she was going to hyperventilate. She struggled to gain control of her breathing and went into the kitchen to find Bella and Dora.

"Can't breathe ..." Maggie managed to say.

"Sit down," Dora insisted. "I'm going to fix you some strong tea."

"Whatever it is," Bella said, "we will work it out together. Take a deep breath. Count to four. Now exhale. 1-2-3-4-5-6-7. There. Do it again."

Both the breathing exercise and the tea helped, and Maggie slowly gained control of her emotions. "I can't imagine what happened to me. I've been through so much worse than this, and here I am falling to pieces."

Dora began to rub small circles on her back. "Honey, it's them hormones. They can make a pregnant elephant cry."

Maggie looked up in alarm.

"I'm not saying you look like one. You're still slender. But that baby is causing all the trouble. You'll be fine."

∽

BY THE FOURTH day after Christmas, the guests were antsy and angry. They wanted good news, and the Weather Channel didn't have any. Things in New Mexico were dire. According to the New Mexico DOT, the snowstorms were coming in waves with a new one dumping several inches before the previous one's yield had melted.

Maggie had gone out to the barn to check on the horses and was wading her way slowly through deep snow back toward the lodge. The sound she heard was too loud to be a snowmobile, and yet nothing but snowmobiles had been making their way in or out in days. She shielded her eyes with her hand against the glare of the sparkling ice crystals reflecting from the sunlight on the snow, and her mouth fell open when she saw a caravan of two big trucks kicking up snow clouds in their wake.

When they stopped in front of the house, she stood there wondering who in the world it could be. She took a few steps closer to the side of the truck and read the green logo on the door: Zarek Industries. Before that could register in her brain, the door opened, and Russell jumped down into the snow.

He looked tall and muscular and masculine and wonderful. Logic and pride told her to stand her ground and let him make the first move, but when she saw the heart-rending tenderness of his gaze, she rushed into his arms.

∽

ONCE INSIDE, he and the three men with him, drank hot coffee while warming up by the fire. There were so many questions to ask.

"How did you get here?" Billy asked. "I thought the road was closed."

"It was. It has been for days. We waited by the barricade, and as soon as they lifted it, off we went." Russell said. His gaze kept returning to Maggie who was moving around the room filling up coffee cups and serving cake. He was trying not to be obvious, but he couldn't get enough of looking at her. He wanted to hold her. He wanted to put his hand on her belly and feel the place where his child lay.

"We've got all kinds of supplies in the trucks," Russell said. "This may all clear up soon, but to be safe, we've got everything you might need. Have you lost power yet?"

"Not once," Bella said. "My Ernesto knew how to build a house."

Russell thought it best not to tell her that the issue was not the structure of the houses. If it happened, the cause would be the power lines that became overloaded with snow and fell to the ground. If that happened, he had brought enough generators for all the cabins and for the lodge itself.

"I know you must be tired," Bella said looking at the three men. "We have a cabin you can sleep in, and Dora has some delicious food in the kitchen."

Russell caught the beautiful old woman's eye and gave her a grateful smile. He was pretty sure she was trying to clear everybody out so that he could be alone with Maggie. That was what he wanted, also. More than anything.

~

AFTER EVERYONE LEFT THE ROOM, he turned to watch Maggie fluttering around like a butterfly. She stacked dishes and placed them on a tray, gathered napkins to throw away, and was about to take them into the kitchen.

"Wait a minute," he said. "That's heavy. I'll carry it."

He took it from her and deposited it on the kitchen counter. When he returned, she had seated herself on the far end of the sofa. Knowing that he was the cause of her discomfort, he hated to see how nervous she was.

"Maggie, I..."

She spoke his name at the same time and gulped hard while hot tears dripped down her cheeks. "Oh, damn these hormones. I never cry!"

"Are you well, Magdalena? Is our baby well?"

"We are both fine," she said. "I have regular checkups, and I am almost at the end of the first trimester. After next week, the odds of an uneventful delivery will increase greatly."

"And, I'm afraid to ask; how is Boney? I didn't see him when I came in."

"He's getting better every day. We keep him down at Billy's and Dora's cabin. It's tough for him to get up and down the stairs here at the lodge. I see him every day. Dora's spoiling him rotten. He will be so excited to see you, Russ."

He smiled that crooked grin, and she sniffed as her eyes filled with new tears. "I thought I was never going to see you again. I will never forgive myself for the things I said to you, Russ. I am so sorry."

He moved close to her on the sofa and took her hand. "You don't need to apologize to me, sweetheart. I'm ashamed that you had to get caught up in the sordid drama of my past."

She gently rested her hand on her belly. "You left us alone for a long time," she said.

"I did, and I have no excuse. For the first couple of weeks, I drank too much and felt sorry for myself."

"What did you do for Thanksgiving?" she asked. "I thought about you all day."

"Cracker Barrel makes a mean chicken fried steak."

"Well, at least one turkey was safe that day." She smiled. "And Christmas?"

"We spent Christmas Eve and Christmas Day in the trucks. We kept hoping they would open the road so I could get here to spend it with you." He took her hand

and held it for a moment. "I'm so sorry I haven't been here with you all this time."

She looked at him but did not respond.

"That reminds me," he said. "Wait here."

He grabbed his coat from the hook and ran out into the cold. When he returned, he had snow on his eyelashes and two boxes in his hands. "This one is for Bella," he said and indicated a long narrow box. "And this one's for you."

She took the small box wrapped in red paper and tied with a green bow.

"Well," he said. "Open it."

She laughed with delight, pulled at the ribbon, and slid the top of the box open. In it lay a silver necklace on black velvet. She took it out and turned it over in her palm. A mother and child were carved inside a silver heart.

"Oh, Russ. It's beautiful," she said. "I love it."

"When you wear it, I want you to remember that I will always love you and our baby."

"We should decide on her name, so you won't keep calling her *baby*."

"How do you know it's a girl?"

She gave him a mysterious smile. "Oh, I know."

"Do you have a name in mind?"

"I do. I want to name her Bella Marie and call her Marie. That's Bella's middle name."

"That's perfect," he said. "I love that old woman, and I love the name Marie."

"Russ, what are you going to do? About your business?"

"Well, that's another thing I've been working on since I last saw you. I've completed most of the paperwork. I'm going to sell my half of the business."

"You what? What will you do now?"

A grin overtook his features. "I'll learn to ski; take Boney fishing; take riding lessons from you; play with Marie."

"What are you saying?" She sounded hesitant. "You're not going back to Albuquerque?"

"Not if you'll have me," he said. Then he dropped to one knee beside her and opened his hand. In it was a beautiful heart-shaped diamond ring.

"If you will please forgive me for failing you when you needed me most, I promise I will never let you down again as long as I live. You could never make me feel trapped, Magdalena. It would be the greatest privilege of my life to marry you and make you my wife. Then, we can start filling up this house with children."

She traced his face with her fingers and leaned in to kiss him. "How many children?" she teased.

"Oh, five or six." He looked at her with a loving question in his eyes, and she nodded *yes* as he placed the ring on her finger.

"That's going to take a lot of practice," she said.

The smile in his eyes contained a sensuous flame. "I'm willing to sacrifice."

~

FROM CHARLENE TESS and Judi Thompson:

The characters in the *Angel Falls* series live in a small town, and their lives are often intertwined. Find out what happens next in Book 2, *Crimson Roses*, when Roddy Eastman takes a stray cat to the veterinarian and is surprised to see that Dr. Pepper Chan just happens to be the girl he had a crush on all through high school.

SCAN THE QR code below and get your copy of *Crimson Roses*.

Read the prequel to the *Angel Falls* Series.
If you enjoyed reading this book in the *Angel Falls* series, we invite you to claim your free copy of the delightful novella, Visions of Love, when seventeen-year-old Bella met her husband Reggie Morales.
https://BookHip.com/KXPLBSD

Thanks so much for reading our book. Please consider leaving us a review on our Amazon book page or on Goodreads. Reviews do not have to summarize the book, and they do not have to be long. We appreciate everyone who takes the time to help us by writing a few words. Reviews are so important and help us enter contests and win awards.

Here are the review links to post your review.
Amazon Book Page
https://amzn.to/3zsPady
Goodreads Book Page
http://bit.ly/3KaFEl7

ABOUT THE AUTHORS

Charlene Tess and Judi Thompson are sisters who live over 1400 miles apart. They combined their two last names into the pen name Tess Thompson and write novels as a team.

Judi Thompson has been writing since her early teens. She lives with her husband, Roger, in Texas. She is a retired supervisor for special education in a local school district.

Charlene Tess is a retired writing teacher and writes educational materials and grammar workbooks. She lives with her husband, Jerry, in Colorado.

CONNECT WITH US ON SOCIAL MEDIA

Read the prequel to the *Angel Falls* Series.
If you enjoyed reading this book in the *Angel Falls* series, we invite you to claim your free copy of the delightful novella, *Visions of Love,* when seventeen-year-old Bella met her husband Reggie Morales.
https://BookHip.com/KXPLBSD
Facebook: https://bit.ly/3GCGoek
Twitter: https://bit.ly/3FDoUx3
Amazon Book Page: https://amzn.to/3dfTfJR
Goodreads Book Page: https://bit.ly/3rpLrbD
Email us: NovelsbyTessThompson@gmail.com

Books by Charlene TESS and Judi THOMPSON
www.amazon.com/author/charlenetess
www.amazon.com/author/judithompson

- **Second Daughter (standalone novel)**
- **Secondhand Hearts series**
- **Dixieland Danger series**
- **Chance O' Brien series**
- **Angel Falls series**
- **Texas Plains romantic comedy series**

Scan the QR code below to claim your copy of *Visions of Love*, a delightful love story, which is a prequel to our Angel Falls series.

Made in the USA
Monee, IL
25 June 2024